PETER'S RETURN

This Large Print Book carries the
Seal of Approval of N.A.V.H.

PETER'S RETURN

Cynthia Cooke

Thorndike Press • Waterville, Maine

Published in 2006 by arrangement with Harlequin Books S.A.

Thorndike Press® Large Print Christian Mystery.

The tree indicium is a trademark of Thorndike Press.

The text of this Large Print edition is unabridged.
Other aspects of the book may vary from the original edition.

Set in 16 pt. Plantin.

Printed in the United States on permanent paper.

Library of Congress Cataloging-in-Publication Data

Cooke, Cynthia.
    Peter's return / by Cynthia Cooke.
       p. cm. — (Faith on the line ; bk. 5) (Thorndike Press large print Christian mystery)
    ISBN 0-7862-8757-8 (lg. print : hc : alk. paper)
    1. Women physicians — Fiction. 2. Americans — Venezuela — Fiction. 3. Intelligence officers — United States — Fiction. 4. Drug traffic — Venezuela — Fiction. 5. Large type books. I. Title. II. Series. III. Series: Thorndike Press large print Christian mystery series.
    PS3603.O578P47 2006
    813'.6—dc22   2006009260

This book is dedicated to my
special friends, Rosanne Falcone and
Margaret Dear, for all your help and
support on this story and to my family
for rearranging their summer to
fit into Mommy's writing schedule.
You are the best! I love you!

Trust in the LORD with all your heart
and lean not on your own understanding;
in all your ways acknowledge Him, and
He will make your paths straight.

Proverbs 3:5–6

Cast of Characters

Peter Vance — His dangerous CIA job and the almost-fatal explosion destroyed his marriage and sent him deep underground for the past three years. But running into Emily at Baltasar Escalante's estate can blow his cover . . . and get them both killed.

Dr. Emily Armstrong — Peter's ex-wife is not the adventurous type . . . so why is the lovely doctor in Venezuela working for Doctors Without Borders?

Baltasar Escalante — The drug lord will do anything to comfort his dying son, including kidnap doctors to ease the boy's suffering.

Snake — Escalante's henchman helps Emily — but for what reason?

Dr. Robert Fletcher — The other doctor from Vance Memorial abducted with Emily. Will he live to see his wife and sons once more?

Chapter One

Caracas, Venezuela

Dr. Emily Armstrong grabbed onto Dr. Robert Fletcher's shoulder. "We've been kidnapped!"

Robert's lips twisted in amusement as he patted her fingers. "Let's not be dramatic, Doctor."

Emily withdrew her hand and leaned back against the seat. "I should have known the moment I saw this black monstrosity of a vehicle with its leather seats and tinted windows that we were in trouble. Only bad guys and government agents drive these things. I know — I was married to one."

"Really?" he said dryly. "I always find it amazing that before the marriage we're Mr. Perfect, Mr. Wonderful, yet after —"

"Not a *bad* guy," she corrected. "A government type." She screwed her lips into a don't-you-know-anything expression, leaned in closer, and lowered her voice. "CIA, if you must know."

"I've heard," Robert replied. "The illustrious missing Peter Vance. Heard he gave it all up and headed for the woods to find himself. What was that, three years ago? You must have done quite a number on him."

Emily snorted, though a pang shot through her. "Peter loved his work, loved the danger. I couldn't see him giving it up for anyone, not even me." She swallowed the lump in her throat and watched the South American city pass by.

"Why give it up? You seem like a girl who likes a little danger in her life."

Emily turned from the tinted window as high-rise apartments gave way to ramshackle shacks, and brushed her long blond hair behind her ear. "Who, me? I don't do danger."

It was Robert's turn to snort.

"What?" she demanded, not sure how he could possibly get the impression from her boring, nothing-ever-happens-to-me life that she could be the type of woman who liked danger.

"If I believed that, even for a second, then you'd be home right now in your safe little apartment, in your idyllic American town and not on your way to a primitive Venezuelan clinic."

Emily lifted her chin in indignation. "I said I don't like danger, I didn't say I don't like helping people. When Kate Montgomery told me about the condition of the poor children living in the *barrios*, how could I not agree to come down here and help?"

"Even after what had happened to Adam?"

"Adam's shooting was an extraordinary circumstance. Dr. Valenti was a desperate man who got himself addicted to pain-killers. Otherwise, I don't believe he ever would have tried to steal drugs from the clinic. But you're right, whatever he got himself into, he got in too deep. Thank the Lord he's a bad shot and Adam survived. In any case, Dr. Valenti was caught and extra security measures at the clinic have been put into place. We shouldn't have to worry about anything like that happening again."

Robert looked grim. "Unfortunately, Valenti was killed in jail so we'll never know the truth of what was behind it all, or who."

"You're looking for conspiracies where they don't exist," Emily said matter-of-factly. "Nothing else could possibly go wrong." But even as she said the words, she realized she was worried. Something didn't feel right, but she couldn't put her finger on exactly what was bothering her. The town? The car? The driver? "Unless of course we've been kidnapped. You know kidnappings are very popular in this region."

Robert's shoulders shook with an unsuppressed chuckle.

"I'm glad you find me so amusing," she said and leaned forward to speak to the driver. "How much longer to the clinic? I thought it was just outside Caracas." She glanced out the window. "We've been outside of Caracas for a while now."

The man didn't respond, just continued driving as if she weren't even there. She couldn't say she liked his looks much, all dark and swarthy with a large coiling red-and-black snake tattooed on his arm.

"Relax," Robert said, nudging her. "We have nothing to worry about. It's a good thing you don't 'do' danger. I have a feeling you wouldn't do it very well." His smile grew wide and generous.

Emily gave him a serious pout. "And what about you? It's not like I'm leaving a family behind. What's your story? Why would you leave Pamela and those two precious sons of yours to come down here?"

"No story, just doing what I do best."

"Ha!" Emily blurted. "Just a small dose of arrogance to go with that cup of ego, Doctor?"

He laughed a hearty sound that reached deep inside his chest. "All right, I confess. This stint on my résumé will do wonders for my career. I'll only be gone three months, not long enough for my family to even miss me."

"Don't count on that."

He nodded, suddenly serious. "I know. I miss them already."

She gave his shoulder a pat, then looked past him out the window and saw a sign for Santa Maria de Flores. "I think we're here."

They continued through the small primitive town, passing run-down houses and barefoot, half-clad children playing in the street. Emily frowned as the driver turned onto a small dirt road on the outskirts of town that led up into the hills. "Is this right? Shouldn't the clinic be back in the town?" Robert looked as nonplussed as she felt. She turned back to the driver. "Excuse me?" she said loudly.

"He probably doesn't understand English," Robert said.

"Con permiso?" she amended. Some-

thing was wrong with this driver. Joking aside, something really had been nagging her ever since she saw him in the airport holding up a Doctors Without Borders sign. Without question, they'd followed him like little lambs to the slaughter. *"Con permiso,"* she said a little more forcefully, and this time tapped the driver's shoulder.

Ignoring her, the driver leaned forward and pushed a button. Before she could take another breath, a clear partition rose between them. Emily looked into Robert's widened eyes. The shocked disbelief on his face would have been comical if it weren't for the sick feeling of dread growing in her stomach. "What are we going to do?" she whispered.

Robert tried to open his door, but it wouldn't budge. Then he tried the window. It, too, was immovable.

"Oh, Lord, protect us," Emily said between breaths that were suddenly coming too fast and too short.

"It's okay, don't panic. I've heard about these guys. If we pay them, they'll let us go. In fact, some are even desperate enough to take a check. Did you bring your checkbook?"

"Checkbook?" she blurted. "That's absurd. Who would I make it out to, Mr. Kidnapper?"

"It's true. I saw it on *20/20.*"

"You're not serious?" Her eyes searched his. *He was.* "Let's pray it will be as simple as that," she muttered.

They didn't say another word as the driver took them deeper into the Venezuelan countryside.

Emily closed her eyes. She wanted to pray, but she couldn't bring herself to do it. It had been so long since she'd been able to connect with the Lord. She'd made a promise, not any ordinary promise, but a deathbed promise to God and she'd broken it. She'd lived with the shame for so long it was almost automatic, almost comfortable. She couldn't go asking for more favors now.

Robert took her hand in his and she held it, thankful for his warmth and friendship. She didn't know what she'd do if she were alone.

"We're going to be okay," he whispered. "You have to believe that."

She nodded. "I know. We have to. We're doctors, we're the good guys. Not only that, we're Americans."

Robert smiled and squeezed her hand before turning back toward the window as the driver veered off onto a gravel road. They were deep in the jungle now, not a sign of civilization in sight. Emily couldn't help wondering where they were being taken and under what kind of conditions they would be forced to live until their ransom was paid. *If* their ransom would be paid.

Don't think like that, she told herself, but the sad fact was she was alone in the world — no husband, no siblings, no family to come to her rescue. She swallowed her despair; she'd dealt with her parents' car accident years ago, but Peter was another matter.

She'd lost touch with him and hadn't seen him — no one had — in a very long time. But if by some miracle of God he'd discovered she was gone, would he come looking for her? Would he care? The realization that she couldn't be sure brought little comfort, only the familiar squeeze of regret. His job, his mission, whatever it was he was working on always came before she did.

"Look!" Robert whispered, interrupting the well-worn path her thoughts were taking.

Emily sat up straighter as glimpses of a large stucco wall came into view. They turned at a bend in the road then stopped before a tall iron gate. The driver nodded to the guard sitting in a booth and the gate swung open. Emily couldn't help but be riveted by the grounds inside the gates.

The parklike setting of benches and statues placed strategically beneath cascading trees surrounding a large duck-laden pond caught her breath. Tucked among the trees were several shrubs trimmed in various animal shapes. Flowers in every shape and size greeted them in a riot of color.

Here and there, she spotted the clay tile roofs of several small out-buildings. She tried to focus through the thick foliage, to get her bearings on the bungalows and see what their use was, but she could only catch scattered glimpses before they disappeared into the jungle. A golf cart passed, but instead of laughing tourists enjoying the eighteenth hole, two guards in tan uniforms with rifles slung over their shoulders watched the Suburban, giving their driver a slight nod as they passed.

They turned right onto a cobblestone road and slowly approached a breathtaking Spanish colonial mansion. Emily leaned into Robert and whispered, "I don't think my checkbook is going to get us out of this one."

"Neither do I," he agreed, and a grim look of futility filled his face. She squeezed his hand as they followed the drive around back and parked in front of a garage larger than the elementary school on the corner of Emily's block back in Colorado Springs. In front of the garage, a series of golf carts were parked next to a bright red Porsche.

"Pinch me, Robert. I think we've just been transported into a *Fantasy Island* rerun," she said, trying to lighten the mood.

"Shh, be serious and be quiet. Let me do all the talking."

"Gladly," she whispered. "And as soon as you get us out of this, I'll try not to remind you how sexist you are being."

"Deal," he grumbled. They watched the driver get out and open their door. "Just where are we?" Robert demanded with more bravado than Emily knew he felt.

"You are the guests of Mr. Escalante," the driver said, then stepped back and waited for them to get out of the car.

Robert stood, but didn't move out of the doorway, effectively blocking her exit. She pushed up on her knees and peeked around him. "I demand you take us to the Doctors Without Borders clinic," he insisted.

The driver tilted his chin down and gave Robert a bone-chilling stare. He gestured toward the mansion. "I suggest you cooperate. It will make your stay here a little more pleasant for all of us, if you do." He stepped around Robert and held out his hand. "Dr. Armstrong."

Robert stepped aside. Without taking the driver's hand, Emily got out of the car. There was something dark and dangerous and almost slithering in the man's eyes. He looked like a man who wouldn't give a second's hesitation to killing them right there on the spot. This was not someone she wanted to touch.

The driver nodded, seeming to accept her slight and said, "Follow me."

Robert started forward and Emily followed close behind. "What do you think they want from us?" she said, leaning forward and whispering in his ear.

"I don't know," he said over his shoulder, "but whatever it is, cooperate."

"Of course I'll cooperate," she muttered. What made him think she wouldn't cooperate? As they walked through the lush grounds, Emily wondered if they could make a run for it. And if they did, how far would they get?

"Mr. Escalante's compound encompasses

over two hundred acres," the driver said as they walked. "At all times, there are guards patrolling every inch of the estate in case you should ever need help."

That answered her question.

He gestured beyond the garages. "Through those trees is the tennis court and swimming pool. There is also a hot tub should you feel the desire to relax your muscles after your long journey."

Somehow she didn't think a hot tub would do the trick. As they walked, Emily tried not to be awed by the beauty of the plants, the orchids and the blooming vines hanging from trees. She sucked in a breath as she caught a glimpse of a red, blue and green macaw unlike any she'd ever seen. "It's the Garden of Eden," she muttered.

"Yeah," Robert agreed. "But watch out for snakes."

The driver turned back and looked at them. The dead emptiness in his eyes curled her toes. "I hate snakes," she whispered, and tried to smother the prickling sensation moving through her.

The man led them into a walled-in, shaded courtyard complete with a mosaic of Spanish tiles and a large fountain. Robert stopped next to an intricate wrought-iron table. "Why have you brought us here?" he demanded, and refused to take another step.

The driver kept walking.

Emily threw Robert a pointed look. "What should we call you?" she asked in her most pleasant and professional voice that barely hid the anxiety squeezing her throat.

The man halted and turned back, his cold, predatory gaze stopping her in her tracks. "Snake."

Emily swallowed. She should have known. She tried to speak, but couldn't. Her tongue was stuck to the roof of her mouth.

He turned away, breaking the contact. Emily was so relieved she followed him without hesitation through the French doors and into a room filled with plush leather sofas and chairs facing a big-screen TV.

"All the luxuries of home," Robert muttered.

Snake stood in the center of the room. "This is where you'll stay." He pointed into another room holding a massive mahogany table. "There is a kitchen for your use through there. Mr. Escalante's chef prepares a meal each evening at six. If he wants you to join him, you will. If not, you may have the meal delivered here by informing Esteban."

"Esteban?" Emily squeaked, finally finding her voice.

A muffled cough sounded behind her. Emily turned. A small dark-haired man bowed his head to her and Robert.

"Anything you need, just ask Esteban. He is here to serve you," Snake said, then turned from the room and headed down the hall.

"At least he's not named after a predator," Emily muttered.

Robert frowned. "Be good."

She smirked and followed Snake down the hall. He opened doors off the main corridor that they passed — the kitchen, a bedroom for Robert, one for her — and still they continued down the hall. Fear and irritation twisted inside her, tightening her muscles and making her tense. She didn't like being kept in the dark, and she certainly didn't like being told what to do. They reached a massive wooden door.

"This will take you back out to the front of the compound," Snake said.

"You mean we can leave whenever we want?" she asked in her most innocent voice. Robert nudged her. She shrugged him off. She was getting tired of not knowing where they were or what was going to happen to them.

"You are free to wander the estate, though I would stick to the cobblestone paths. After all, we are in the middle of a jungle." He turned and headed back down the hall.

Emily stared after him. "And what exactly was that supposed to mean?" she asked Robert.

"Exactly what it sounded like," Robert said. "Wander too far and you'll be eaten."

She took one last look at the door before following them back into the main room. Still, she might just prefer to take her chances in the jungle.

"Mr. Escalante will be with you shortly," Snake said, then left the room.

Emily let out a sigh of relief as he disappeared from her view, then turned to Robert. "Do you think this Escalante guy is in charge of the Doctors Without Borders program? Is that why we're here?"

"Would be nice, but I doubt it."

So did she, but she couldn't help hoping. "What kind of a name is Snake anyway? Why do you think they call him that?"

"Maybe his bite is poisonous," Robert said as he studied the grounds outside the windows.

"Yeah, or maybe he can squeeze the life out of you with his monstrous hands."

Robert turned to her, his eyebrows raised.

She got up and started to pace. "I've been kidnapped and brought to paradise by a man named Snake and I have no idea why, or what's going to happen next, or if I'm going to get to go home, or live, or breathe ever again."

Robert walked over to her and patted her back. "You're hyperventilating."

"I am not!" she insisted.

He cocked an eyebrow that reminded her of an indulgent father reprimanding his young.

She couldn't say she liked it much. "All right, maybe I am . . . just a little." She didn't know if she heard his approach or if she just felt his dark stare, but she turned to find a large man filling the doorway. Once he had their attention, he strode into the room with the casual ease and confidence of a general commanding his troops.

"Dr. Fletcher, Dr. Armstrong, thank you for coming. I'm most appreciative of your help," he greeted in a strong booming voice.

"We weren't given much choice," Robert said. "Mr. . . . ?"

"Escalante. But, please, call me Baltasar. I'm sorry if we worried you. Circumstances dictated the necessary action. I assume your drive from Caracas was comfortable?"

"Why exactly are we here?" Emily asked abruptly, somewhat disconcerted by his slicked, black hair or perhaps it was his piercing gaze; either way her skin was crawling.

Baltasar's eyes met hers and pinned her to the floor. "I need you to help my son." He sat on one of the long leather sofas, leaned forward and rested his elbows on his knees. "If I may get to the point, my son, Marcos, is very sick. I'm afraid he's dying. I need your help to make his last days as comfortable for him as possible."

Emily took a deep breath and sat in a chair nearby.

"He is my only child," Baltasar continued. "I love him greatly and can't stand to see him suffer."

The pain widening his eyes gave Emily's heart an uncomfortable squeeze. Against her will, she softened toward the man. But only a little.

"I will make it worth your while," he said with a great deal of sincerity.

Emily couldn't help wondering how much of it was real. He was obviously a man who knew what he wanted and exactly how to get it. "Of course we can help your son," she responded, trying to maintain a professional distance. "That's why

Dr. Fletcher and I came here, to help the children."

He gave her a warm smile.

"But," she added, and couldn't help cringing as his smile stiffened. "As beautiful as your estate is, we'd prefer to help your son at the clinic in Santa Maria de Flores."

"I'm afraid Marcos can't be moved," Baltasar said, standing. "Now, please, come and meet my son."

His gaze slid over her, sizing her up. She couldn't say she liked it.

"If you don't mind, Mr. Escalante," Robert said without making a move to join him at the door. "What exactly is your son's illness?"

"Marcos was born HIV-positive, which has been further complicated by his hemophilia. I'm afraid his illness has progressed to AIDS. It's been very difficult for all of us and after he lost his last doctor . . . well, you can see why I'd view a pediatric hematologist with Dr. Armstrong's impeccable credentials as a blessing, and her arrival here in Venezuela as a gift from God Himself. What better doctors could He have sent than the two of you to look after my son?"

Emily blinked. She understood the pain

26

parents of terminally ill children suffered, but hoped he wasn't reading more into their presence than there was. They were doctors, not miracle workers. "Dr. Fletcher and I will do whatever we can to help Marcos. I'm truly sorry for what you've had to go through, and for the difficult road that lies ahead for your family."

Baltasar smiled, took her arm, and wrapped it around his own. "You, Dr. Armstrong, are an angel."

Either that or a tremendous fool, she thought. She set her mind to focusing on the child as they walked down the hall, and not on their predicament. As they entered the room, Emily was surprised to see it rivaled any at Vance Memorial back in Colorado Springs. Mr. Escalante had provided his son with the best medical equipment available.

"Will you have everything here that you need?" he asked.

"More than enough," Emily said, looking around. A side door opened and a woman dressed in a nurse's uniform walked in pushing a little boy in a wheelchair. His emaciated body didn't detract from the love and laughter in his large brown eyes. "Papa!" he greeted.

"Hello, Marcos." Baltasar knelt down to

27

be at eye level with his son. "I'd like you to meet your new doctors. This is Dr. Armstrong and Dr. Fletcher."

"Buenas tardes," Marcos said.

Emily smiled. "Good afternoon to you, Marcos."

Baltasar stood. "And this is Marcos's nurse, Marguerite."

The nurse smiled pleasantly then walked over to Marcos's hospital bed and turned down the covers.

"Mr. Escalante —"

"Baltasar, please."

Emily gave a slight nod. "Baltasar, do you have Marcos's medical records for us to look at?"

He looked pleased at her question. "Absolutely, right over here." He opened up a drawer and removed a thick file. Emily took it from him. "Please read it over, visit with my son, and then let me know your findings at dinner this evening."

Emily got the feeling his offer wasn't a request.

He kissed Marcos on the head and left the room. After the nurse settled Marcos into his bed, Emily stepped forward. "How are you feeling?" she asked the boy.

"Okay," he said, then started to cough.

As his coughing persisted, she asked the

nurse for a stethoscope and thermometer. She took his temperature, frowned as she read the elevated reading, then listened to his chest. His little face filled with fatigue. Emily's gaze met Robert's across the bed. "Lay back and get some rest," she said softly to the child, gently brushing his forehead with her fingertips.

He nodded and gave her a sleepy smile that tugged at her heart. Of all the terminally ill children she'd had to help, she'd never gotten used to the pain and heartache that came with each one she lost. She knew she should distance herself from them, but then she'd look into their sweet, innocent, scared eyes and she'd be lost, her heart sunk. Each time, she'd hoped God in His infinite wisdom and mercy would spare them. Maybe this time He would. She gave Marcos a warm smile, then joined Robert and the nurse in the outer room.

"How long has he been coughing?" Emily asked the nurse.

"He just started this morning."

"There's moisture and rattling in his chest. He's in the beginning stages of pneumonia." Emily had seen it many times before, and as the illness progressed, the child would grow weaker and weaker.

"Mr. Escalante will need to be told," Marguerite said while reaching into an overhead cabinet.

"What happened to Marcos's last doctor?" Robert asked casually. Emily had wondered the same thing. She recalled Baltasar's earlier reference to losing Marcos's doctor, but couldn't imagine a doctor leaving his patient at this stage in his illness. And Baltasar didn't seem like the sort of man who would just let him go.

The nurse mumbled something without turning.

"I'm sorry, what was that?" Emily asked.

Marguerite pulled out a syringe and bottle of antibiotics, then said, "Snakebite," and quickly left the room.

Emily turned to Robert. Uneasiness tweaked her stomach as she held his gaze. "There is way too much talk about snakes around here."

Peter Vance took in his surroundings and hoped his years of hard work had paid off and he'd finally been granted access into the heart of La Mano Oscura, also known as The Dark Hand. The manicured grounds were a stark contrast to the un-tamed jungle pushing at the compound's tall stone walls. The bungalow he'd been led to was large and gracious, with ceiling fans, plantation shutters and yards of mosquito netting. It sure beat the shack he'd been living in — he could barely call it a shack — since he'd left Colorado Springs three years ago.

He knew when the CIA asked him to upgrade his status and go deep undercover as an operations officer, life as he knew it would be over. But he hadn't expected how much the isolation would bother him, or how much he'd miss his family.

How much he'd miss Emily.

He shook off the thought as he had numerous times before. He'd hoped the long nights alone would have purged her from his mind. Unfortunately they hadn't. Even here deep in the jungles of Venezuela, where nary the sight of a long wheat-colored blonde could be found, he'd see something that would remind him of the exact shade of hazel in her eyes and there she'd be, at the forefront of his mind.

Somehow, some way, he had to forget her and move on. By now she'd probably found herself a nice doctor husband, one who'd come home to her safe and sound every night and given her lots of drooling babies to take care of. He could see it perfectly in his mind, the type of life she'd longed for, the type of life he could never give her.

He took out his secured satellite phone and dialed Maxwell Vance, his father and case handler.

"You at the compound?" Max asked as he picked up the line.

"Affirmative."

"Good. We've had a major break on this end. It won't be long now."

Peter sighed and allowed himself a second to hope. Three years without a break, a vacation or a meal from his mother's diner, The Stagecoach Café. How he wished he could go home and see everyone even if it was only for a day.

"We've uncovered an air force connection to Diablo."

He raised his eyebrows. The air force is connected with Colorado Springs' major crime syndicate? No wonder they had such a hard time tackling their problems. "Is La Mano Oscura Diablo's main supplier?"

"Affirmative. If everything goes according to plan, the sting we've set in motion should bring the Venezuelan cartel to its knees. All your hard work is finally going to pay off. You're in the perfect position to help us bring La Mano Oscura down."

"It's all I think about, believe me."

"If you can, get the names of any operatives still set up here in Colorado that we may have missed. We can't afford for Escalante to get wind of our plans."

"Got it."

"Also, Barclay has taken a tumble."

Peter shouldn't have been surprised. They had suspected that hotel tycoon Alistair Barclay was the kingpin of the Diablo organization credited with the increase of drug trafficking to hit Colorado Springs, but they hadn't been able to get the goods on him. Things were looking up.

"Has he confirmed Escalante is *El Patrón?*" Peter asked. They'd been hoping for something to pinpoint Escalante as the head of La Mano Oscura, but they hadn't had much luck. "I know in my gut he's our guy, but he's kept himself clean and surrounded with well-established, legitimate connections. Has he found out about Barclay's arrest?"

"Negative, as far as we know. He's expecting a shipment through General Hadley of cash and high-definition Keyhole Satellite images of his lab on the Colombian border. Expect company in place of the shipment. The operation will go down on the thirteenth at zero-hundred hours. Make sure you're there. We'll need you to help tie up any loose ends. This could be it."

Peter took a deep breath and tried not to let himself hope. He wanted to leave, but wasn't sure what he'd do next. The jungle and his cover as Pietro Presti had been a part of him for so long, he wasn't sure how he could ever go back to just being Peter Vance. He glanced out the window and saw Escalante heading toward the bungalow down the main path. "Escalante's coming, I've got to go."

"Wait . . . there's one more thing you should know."

Peter heard the trepidation in his father's voice, a voice he knew well enough to know this wasn't something he wanted to hear. This was something personal. His gut tightened.

"It's about Emily. . . ."

Emily.

"Mr. Presti?" Baltasar Escalante said as he walked through the opened door.

Peter disconnected the line and turned, the name of his ex-wife ringing in his ear.

Chapter Two

Determination overrode emotion. For three years, Peter had worked hard to establish his cover as small-time drug trafficker Pietro Presti hoping to gain the attention of *El Patrón,* kingpin of La Mano Oscura. Now was his chance. He was in the perfect position to find out the truth about Baltasar Escalante and his connection to La Mano Oscura. He had to stay focused. He couldn't afford to let himself wonder about Emily and what his father wanted to tell him about her.

"Mr. Presti, how do you like your quarters?" Baltasar asked as he strolled into the room.

"Very much," Peter responded. "Thank you for your hospitality and please, my friends call me Pietro."

"Pietro it is," Baltasar said, and sat in a teal-and-salmon chair. He rested his long arms against the bamboo trim and watched Peter for a disquieting second. His lips curved into a small, predatory smile. "I hope I didn't interrupt your phone call?"

Peter forced a casual air. "Not at all, just checking on a few business deals."

As Baltasar continued to stare at him, Peter hoped the invitation to the compound would turn out to be a friendly one.

"I understand you've been having some run-ins with our mutual acquaintance, Domingo," Baltasar finally said.

Peter held up his hands, palms out, then gave a gentle shake of his head. "I'm just a small-time guy trying to eke out a living in a big-time jungle. Domingo has taken issue with some of my methods."

Baltasar nodded, his dark eyes narrowing in contemplation. "I understand perfectly. Let's take a walk," he said, rising. "There's something I want to show you."

Peter followed him out the door, knowing full well when he received Baltasar's summons it could mean trouble. He'd taken a chance stirring up the pot with Domingo, but he needed to gain Baltasar's notice. The few days he'd taken to scope out the perimeter of the compound and stash a motorcycle in a strategic location outside the wall could pay off sooner than he'd thought.

In silence, they walked through the gardens on a cobblestone path moving far away from the main house.

"Your estate is incredible," Peter said truthfully, trying to gauge Baltasar's mood.

"I enjoy nice things. I work hard to achieve them. You can, too, if you play according to the rules." Baltasar looked at him out of the corner of his eye.

His gamble with Domingo had been the right one. Now they were getting somewhere. "Rules have never been my strong suit," Peter said casually, but laced his tone with an edge of steel.

"I've noticed. But to succeed in La Mano Oscura, one must never tread too far off the beaten path."

Peter contemplated his response, but stopped as the snarl of a wild cat pricked the hairs on the nape of his neck. Slowly, he turned toward the tree closest to the path. A midnight-black jaguar with yellow-green eyes watching his every move sat on a low tree branch, its tail twitching, a low growl resonating deep in its chest. Peter's breath knotted in his throat. He'd seen firsthand what a cat that size could do to a man, and it wasn't a pretty sight.

Baltasar approached the cat, reached up and rubbed its head. "Hello, Akisha," he cooed. He took a napkin out of his pocket, then carefully removed a large piece of raw meat and fed it to the cat. He turned back to Peter. "As I was saying, veering too far off the path might not be a healthy choice."

Stunned, Peter could only nod as he watched the cat devour his treat. He expelled a relieved breath as they turned and headed back down the path toward the main house. He was still groping to get a handle on whether this visit would be agreeable to him when Baltasar said, "I love Venezuela. My enterprises have taken me many places, Pietro, and yet I always come back home where the colors are vibrant and the smell of the jungle heightens your senses."

"I believe you have the makings of a poet, Mr. Escalante," Peter said after a moment's hesitation.

Baltasar let loose a deep, barrel-chested laugh. "My dear late wife used to say the same thing." He shook his head. "How I miss her. You married?"

"Once," Peter answered. "Unfortunately, it didn't work out."

"It takes a special kind of woman to be married to men like us." Baltasar patted him on the back and as they approached the main house he led him through a set of French doors into a comfortable yet masculine office.

Peter casually scanned the room, taking in the deep brown leather sofa flanked by two overstuffed chairs. Against the far wall, but still maintaining the focal point of the room, was a large cherrywood desk and credenza. Everything he would need to unearth Baltasar's nefarious activities would probably be found in that monstrous desk.

"We can talk privately here," Baltasar said, and took a seat behind the desk.

Peter viewed this as a good sign. If Baltasar had wanted bloodshed, he wouldn't have brought him into a room sporting a plush Turkish carpet. And they wouldn't be alone. Baltasar opened a small humidor sitting atop his desk, pulled out a rich brown cigar, and gestured to Peter.

Peter didn't care for cigars, but he knew it would be bad form to refuse. He nodded and watched as Baltasar used a stainless steel cutter to neatly snip off the cigar's end before passing it to him. Peter accepted Baltasar's offer and held it under his nose, breathing deep its strong aroma, and then waited for the business to begin.

"Along with your aversion to rules," Baltasar said after lighting and inhaling deeply off his cigar. He rolled the smoke around in his mouth before exhaling and finishing his thought. "Your reputation as an innovator and a man of action precedes you. I can use someone like that in my organization. You interested?"

Peter took a deep drag off the cigar and let Baltasar stew a moment, then said, "Perhaps. Depends on what you have in mind."

Baltasar held his gaze. "Right now I'm in a position to expand my operations and I need someone in the States to head it up for me. You are an American, *sí?*"

Peter nodded and gestured with the cigar. "But you already knew that. You see, your reputation precedes you, too, Mr. Escalante, and I know you wouldn't have brought me here if you didn't already know everything there was to know about me."

Baltasar smiled, his expression moving from benign indulgence to sharp respect. "Good, then we can drop the pretenses?"

"Please do." Peter leaned back in the chair.

"I know you're good at what you do. I know you're considered a bit of a hothead. I also know you're American, and a trip back home might not be such a bad idea, since our mutual friend Domingo isn't too enamored with you at the moment."

"Domingo is a fool," Peter countered.

"He doesn't have the foresight, the imagination, or the guts to run an organization that will have the success and the reputation of La Mano Oscura."

Baltasar nodded, his fingers coming together to steeple beneath his chin. "I appreciate the compliment."

Bingo. Baltasar was indeed *El Patrón,* leader of La Mano Oscura.

"But I didn't bring you here to hear compliments, Pietro. Personally, I could care less if Domingo hacks you up and feeds you to his beloved crocodiles. But I believe you can help me and if you turn out to be worth my trouble, then you'll get a free ticket back to Chicago and a piece of the La Mano Oscura pie. You interested?"

"Perhaps. How big a piece?" Peter asked, and couldn't help flashing a predatory smile of his own.

Baltasar laughed. "I think I could like you, Pietro." He was silent for a moment, his fingers tapping out a simple beat on his desk. "I know you have a small but well-run organization in Chicago. How would you feel about expanding that operation?"

"Depends if the returns are as big as the risk. I like to stay small because it keeps me under the authority's radar."

"It also keeps you living in shacks in the jungle."

Peter snuffed out his cigar in a crystal ashtray. "You got me there."

"I'm expecting a large payment soon that will cover all the expenses necessary to set you up properly. I have one thousand kilos of pure powder processed and ready. I can have half that shipment sent to Chicago. Can you handle it?"

"I can, but I'll have to increase my base."

"Think you can have it done by the thirteenth?"

Peter nodded. "Absolutely."

"Good. I'm cutting back on my organization in Colorado. I want to transfer operations to Chicago consecutively."

Peter schooled his features not to show too much excitement. This was a bigger break than any of them had anticipated. Baltasar must be very unhappy with Barclay to be cutting him out. Either that or he was on to Barclay's arrest. And if that was the case, this whole conversation could be a setup and Baltasar could have wind of the sting operation the CIA had planned.

Peter's stomach turned, and it wasn't just from the cigar.

"All communications will be directly between you and I. You won't use my name,

but will always refer to me as *El Patrón.*
Each month I will send an e-mail communication of when you can expect the next shipment of kilos and where —"

The door burst open and a woman rushed in, her long, flowing wheat-gold hair, bouncing across her shoulders.

Baltasar stood.

The woman stopped dead in her tracks, her arms frozen in midswing, her large hazel eyes staring in widened shock. At him.

Emily.

Peter's heart slammed into the side of his chest.

A man dressed in the tan uniform of Baltasar's guards came running up behind her, grabbed her by the arm, and pulled her back.

Peter stood, and had to stop himself from rushing forward and ripping the man's arm off. He must be dreaming. It couldn't possibly be *his* Emily standing in Baltasar Escalante's office being manhandled by a guard.

"I am so sorry, Mr. Escalante," the guard said. "The *señorita* is faster than she looks." His lips quivered in disgust. "I won't let her get by me again."

Emily's shocked gaze hadn't left Peter's.

It was her. And if he didn't do something fast, she would say or do something, and the jig would be up, his cover blown.

"It's all right, Esteban," Baltasar said, and walked toward them. "You may leave us." He made a sweeping gesture with his arm. The guard nodded and backed out the door. Peter took advantage of Baltasar's diverted attention and held a forefinger to his lips. For a brief second, Emily's eyes widened.

Once the door clicked shut, Baltasar turned back to Emily. His Emily. What was she doing there? Why wasn't she back home in Colorado Springs working at Vance Memorial and raising babies? His mind felt wrapped in several layers of cotton. He forced out three quick breaths, then took a deep one and tried not to think about how fast his heart was beating. He had to calm down. He had to make sure neither one of them gave the game away.

Baltasar turned back to his desk and snuffed out his cigar. "Dr. Armstrong, is everything all right with Marcos?" he asked.

Emily still hadn't spoken. She just stood there staring, her emotions playing across her face — shock, pain, regret.

Peter held his breath. *Come on, Emily.*

Pull it together. Don't give me away.

"Dr. Armstrong?" Baltasar said again.

Peter didn't like the way Baltasar's gaze kept shifting from her to him then back to her again.

"Is everything all right?" he asked again.

She took a step toward Peter, her mouth opening to speak. He lifted his hand a fraction of an inch, gave a slight shake of his head, and hoped she could still read him as easily as he could still read her.

"Sorry," she said, regaining her voice, though it was obvious how much of a struggle it was for her.

"Is everything all right with Marcos?" Speculation ran high in Baltasar's tone.

Peter turned toward the window, breaking their connection before Baltasar's speculation turned to suspicion.

"Yes. I'm sorry," Emily said, seeming to pull it together. "I didn't mean to frighten you. Marcos is coming down with a cough that we'll need to keep a close watch on. It seems he's developed pneumonia. But he's been given antibiotics. His spirits are high and he's resting comfortably."

Peter sat back in his chair and acted uninterested while watching them out of the corner of his eye. He knew Baltasar's son was dying of AIDS, which explained why

45

Emily, a pediatric hematologist, would be there, but it certainly didn't explain *how* she got there.

"He's a wonderful little boy," Emily added.

"Thank you," Baltasar said softly. "I think so, too."

She fell silent, her large hazel eyes once again seeking out Peter's, once again causing a painful lurch in his chest. He tried not to look at her, tried to look back out the window, or at the desk, anywhere, but all the willpower in the world couldn't pull him away. How he missed her, the sharp pain of it sliced through him.

"Was there something you needed, Dr. Armstrong?"

The abrupt edge to Baltasar's tone sent a twinge of anxiety rushing through him. They'd have to be careful around this man. From everything Peter had heard and seen, he could play Mr. Charm, but underneath he was a diabolical and ruthless killer.

"Yes," Emily said, and turned slightly, giving Baltasar her full attention.

That's it, babe. Don't let him see you sweat.

"The phones in our wing aren't working and we need to call the clinic and let them know we've arrived safely. It's been several hours since we were due and we don't want them to worry."

"That's very thoughtful of you, Dr. Armstrong, but I've already contacted the clinic and let them know you've been delayed."

As she hesitated, the pieces clicked into place. Baltasar needed a doctor for his son and he took one, regardless of what she wanted or needed, or who might need her. *Come on, baby. Play it cool. This isn't Mr. Altruistic; this is a monster in disguise.*

"And then there's the matter of Dr. Fletcher's wife and children. They were expecting to hear from him. They must be worried sick."

Dr. Fletcher. Peter vaguely recalled that name from Vance Memorial's Christmas parties.

Baltasar smiled warmly. "Of course they are. We must alleviate their worry. Tell Dr. Fletcher to post a letter and I'll see it's mailed immediately. I'm sorry, but our phone service is sporadic at best, and it isn't working right now. I'll make sure you and Dr. Fletcher know the minute it comes back on."

Emily's shoulders fell with her relief. "Thank you, Mr. Escalante. We really appreciate it."

"Please, my name is Baltasar. And thank *you.* There's no way I could ever express the appreciation I feel toward you and the good Dr. Fletcher. This is the least I can do." Baltasar turned toward the door and called for Esteban.

The guard stuck his head in the room. *"Sí?"*

"Please see Dr. Armstrong back to the hospital wing."

"Yes, sir." He stepped into the room and took Emily's arm.

Frustrated by his inability to intercede, Peter opened his mouth to protest, then forced himself to close it again as the guard led her out of the room. A fist of dread grabbed hold of Peter's solar plexus and gave a firm squeeze. She was a giant monkey wrench that could totally screw up his operation. But didn't she look good? Better than he remembered. And if he closed his eyes, he was sure he could recall what she smelled like, and how her skin would feel as soft as silk beneath his touch.

"I'm sorry for the interruption," Baltasar said, shaking his head and sitting back down behind his desk. "My son's new doctor. I don't think she heard much, but I do think she's going to give me trouble."

Peter raised his eyebrows but didn't say

anything, hoping the man would continue, but not wanting to appear too interested.

Baltasar leaned back in his chair and stared at him. "I manage to stay one step ahead of the game by not allowing mistakes or mishaps of any kind. There's too much at stake here for us to take unnecessary chances or risks."

Was he talking about Emily or him? Either way wasn't good. With a modicum of indifference in his tone, Peter asked, "Is the doctor a risk?"

"She has too much backbone for a woman. She's trouble. I can feel it right here." With a tight fist, he punched his gut.

The cold ferocity in his gaze sent a sliver of fear arcing through Peter's mind. He wished he could jump out of his chair, find Emily and get her out of Venezuela. But he couldn't jeopardize his mission — too much was at stake. Peter forced himself to concentrate on the man, and on his job.

"My associates and I have a network of hotels in Chicago on the river," Baltasar said, leaning back in his chair and replacing the snubbed out cigar in his mouth. "I will have a shipment of say two hundred kilos divided up and delivered to four hotels at noon tomorrow." He took out a pad of paper and wrote down the

49

names and addresses of the hotels. "Have your people in place to pick up the shipments. If there's a problem, or a leak of any kind, I will know it came from your end. Make sure that doesn't happen, or our relationship will come to an abrupt end and I can assure you it won't be pretty."

Peter sucked up a breath and squared his shoulders. "No problem, Mr. Escalante. I don't do pretty. My people know what's at stake."

And so did he. Only now there was a lot more at stake than nailing a drug lord. Now he had to rescue his ex-wife and if he knew Emily, she wouldn't make it easy.

After leaving Baltasar's office, Emily tried to walk down the hall as if she didn't have a thing on her mind other than Marcos, but she was having trouble feeling her legs. Peter was alive and well right there in Venezuela. And looking like a vision out of an action movie.

She wasn't sure how she'd recognized him with that long, shaggy, dark hair and scruffy morning — no, make that afternoon shadow. Who was she kidding? She would have known those ice-blue eyes anywhere. With one look, they pierced her soul and set her heart on fire.

Peter. His name whispered across her mind. She smiled, her heart filling with hope and anticipation even though Esteban was furiously hissing who-knew-what in Spanish behind her. Suddenly he grabbed her arm. She bit her lip as his long bony fingers dug into her flesh, then cried out as he slammed her against the wall.

"Don't ever do that to me again, *chiquita,* or you will be one sorry little lady doctor." He was too close to her, his raspy, garlic breath fanning her cheek. "Such soft, tender skin, white and fine as porcelain," he breathed. "The kind of skin that bruises easily." He ran a calloused finger down her cheek. "Even in places that can't be seen, eh?"

Nausea turned her stomach, yet she stared him down, wide-eyed and boldly refusing to let him see her fear. He was nothing more than a bully, a low-man-on-the-totem-pole bully who wanted to make her feel afraid. She wouldn't give him the satisfaction.

Without flinching she held his gaze and lifted her chin. "If you don't mind, *Esteban,* I need to get back to Marcos. Unless you want me to inform Mr. Escalante how you've detained me when I meet him for dinner tonight."

Esteban's eyes narrowed, quickening the

blood coursing through her body. "Don't push me, *chiquita.*"

"What's going on here?" Snake asked as he rounded the corner.

Emily had never been more relieved to see a thug in her life. "I'm afraid I've upset Esteban," she said, and casually stepped out from the wall and beyond his touch. The look crossing Snake's face had her clamping down on her jaw to keep her teeth from rattling. Lord, if he wasn't the scariest man she'd ever met.

"Dr. Armstrong interrupted Mr. Baltasar," Esteban explained. "She needs to understand she will be punished if she does it again."

"I'll walk Dr. Armstrong back to her wing," Snake said, looking at his watch. "I'm sure she won't need you again until morning."

Esteban glared at her, muttered a few more words in Spanish, then disappeared down the hall.

Emily turned to Snake. "Thank you. I'm afraid that man has control issues."

"Is something wrong with Marcos?" he asked, his eyes narrowing in speculation.

"I wanted to use the phone," she said, feeling the need to explain herself and not liking it.

He looked at her like she had the brains of a snail. "Make sure you don't pop in on Mr. Escalante unannounced again. It wouldn't be healthy," Snake said evenly. Something in his tone, in his expression, scared her more than the quivering, unhinged Esteban.

"Do you think it's possible to get someone else to 'serve' us other than Esteban?"

"No," he said, then gestured her forward.

"Great," she muttered, and let him lead her back down the hall to the hospital wing. Where was she and who exactly was Mr. Baltasar Escalante? And what did *he* have to do with Peter?

They had been talking quite seriously when she'd walked in, something about kilos. Emily stiffened as the word ran through her mind. She could no longer ignore the trepidation skittering down her spine. There was only one thing she knew of that came in kilos. *Drugs.*

She stole a glance behind her at Snake. Why hadn't she seen it before? They weren't the guests of an eccentric millionaire worried about his son; they were the prisoners of a drug lord. A cold sweat washed over her. What did that say about Peter?

When they reached the hospital wing, Emily sat on the sofa and tried to still her pounding heart. Is this where Peter has been for the past three years? Why hadn't he called anyone? Why hadn't he cared that no one had known whether he was dead or alive? Her shoulders sagged as she dropped her face in her hands.

She hadn't let herself dwell on it, hadn't wanted to face the implications of such a sustained absence. A part of her hoped he was alive, but she hadn't known for sure. Now she did. But was he trafficking in drugs?

She thought of all the damage drugs did to the users and their families and all the problems they'd had in Colorado Springs lately — the increase in victims of violence at the Galilee Women's Shelter and all the overdoses at the hospital. She sighed. No, the Peter she knew could never be involved with drugs. Maybe he was still with the CIA? He could be working undercover, that would explain why no one had heard from him for so long. And why he didn't want Baltasar to know they knew each other. Either scenario meant he wouldn't be much help to her and Robert. She would always come second to his job, no matter what it was. She always had.

She thought back to their marriage and how much she'd loved him, and the more she loved him the more afraid she'd grown as he became more and more entranced with his job. She knew it wouldn't have been long before he'd be working under-cover, going on dangerous assignments and getting himself killed. The explosion that put him in the hospital was a real eye-opener for her, and she knew she couldn't live that way — always wondering, always worrying.

She'd made an impulsive and emotional decision to walk out on their marriage. Then she'd waited for him to come home and tell her how foolish she'd been, to as-sure her that he'd be fine, that he wouldn't take unnecessary risks, that he wouldn't put his job before their marriage. But he never came. He hadn't loved her enough to fight for her. He accepted her reasons and let her walk away, even though it was the last thing she wanted. Tears stung the back of her eyes. No, as always, she was on her own.

"Emily?"

She opened her eyes to find Robert staring down at her.

"Is everything all right?"

She shook her head, but couldn't find

the words to speak. *Peter is here.* She wished she could tell him, but she'd been the wife of a CIA agent long enough to know better. She patted the couch next to her. After he sat, she leaned in close and whispered in his ear. "I believe Escalante is a drug lord."

"What?"

"I heard him talking about kilos. We have to get out of here."

"I agree, but how?"

"I don't know." Certainly not by counting on Peter. He hadn't even batted an eye at seeing her again. The tears she'd been trying so desperately to keep at bay flooded her eyes. Peter had been her husband. She should be able to count on his help. She should be able to depend on him.

Robert placed an arm around her shoulders and gave her a gentle squeeze. "It's going to be all right. God will hear our prayers."

"I hope so," she whispered, but somehow she didn't think He was listening.

Chapter Three

At that moment, a bout of coughing had Emily rushing into Marcos's room, driving home her point more. If God was there for people, if He listened to their prayers, *her* prayers, how could He let such suffering happen to those the least deserving — the young and innocent? She checked the boy's chart and saw that he'd already been given his medicine. There wasn't much she could do for him. She took his temperature then had him sit up as she handed him a glass of water.

"Thank you, Dr. *Señorita,*" the boy said.

"You're welcome." She watched him finish the water then took the glass from him.

His coughing abated and he gave her a big toothy grin. "I have a loose tooth."

"You do?"

"Uh-huh. See?" He stuck his finger in his mouth and wiggled an incisor.

"Look at that," she said with a big smile. "You have a loose tooth."

He nodded in happy agreement. "Do

you have children?" he asked with eager-
ness lighting his big brown eyes.

His question poked a wound that would
never heal. "No, *pequeño.* No children. If
I did, then I wouldn't have time for all my
children patients."

"Then it is good, no?"

She smiled at him. "It is good. Now
close your eyes and try to get some rest."

He nodded. "I am extra tired today," he
said as his eyes drifted closed.

The poor boy was getting worse by the
hour. Emily sat by his bedside and held his
hand, thinking how unfair it was that he
should have to spend his day in bed.
Children should be running and playing
and driving their parents crazy with their
unrelenting energy.

She gave herself a mental shake. She was
being absurd. Seeing Peter had brought
back all the painful feelings of fear and loss
and wanting a child more than she wanted
her next breath. She sighed. It wasn't
meant to be. It couldn't be. She couldn't
live with a man who put danger and his
work before her. Never again. She had
loved him too much to watch him die. And
he hadn't loved her enough to try something different, something new.

She pulled the sheet up to Marcos's

chest. It didn't matter now. She was over Peter and had been for a long time. The wallop her heart had taken when she saw him earlier was only her feeling of relief that he was still alive, nothing more. She should be thankful and put him out of her mind.

She brushed the hair back from Marcos's forehead. The poor boy was so thin and pale. Each breath was a struggle for him to take. He was in the beginning stages of Pneumocystis carinii pneumonia, an opportunistic infection that had stolen in to take advantage of his shattered immune system.

"Dr. *Señorita?*" He opened his sleepy eyes.

She smiled at him. "I thought you were going to rest."

"Will you pray with me?"

She hesitated.

"My mama used to pray with me. Every day we'd pray together and ask God to watch over us. And every night before I went to sleep, but ever since she died —" His words broke off and pain filled his eyes.

"Of course, I'll pray with you," she said. She couldn't stand to see the heartache filling his little face.

"Papa doesn't pray anymore," he said. "He's mad at God for my disease, he doesn't understand it's not God's fault."

Emily squeezed his hand. "Your papa loves you so much, it hurts him to see you sick. I'm sure he doesn't want you to see him sad."

Marcos's lips trembled as he smiled. "You must be a very smart lady."

"I like to think so."

"My mama would have liked you."

His words tugged at her heart and tightened her throat. "She must have been a wonderful lady to have such a special boy."

He smiled with all the sweetness and optimism that eight-year-olds hold close to their hearts, then pushed his hands together.

"Do you have a favorite prayer?" she asked, hoping he didn't want her to come up with one. It had been so long since she'd prayed, she wasn't sure she could remember the words.

He nodded.

"Okay, then, let's hear it."

He squeezed his eyes shut so hard that his cheeks compressed and his small mouth straightened into a thin, serious line. As Emily watched him, pure joy filled her heart. He was such a treasure. His little voice, weak and tired, sounded crystal clear like the first drops of rain on a cool fall morning. She sat up straighter to listen.

"Dear Lord, now it's time for me to rest, today I tried to do my best. Watch over me as I lie in sleep, help me to have faith in Thee. Care for all the world's little children, the sick and the poor, give them Your blessing. Care for Dr. Armstrong and Dr. Fletcher and Papa the same, this I pray in Jesus's name. Amen."

His big brown eyes opened, capturing hers, and from that moment on her heart was lost.

"You're supposed to say 'Amen,'" he whispered.

"Amen," she said quickly.

He gave a triumphant smile and she rustled his hair. "Are you ready to go to sleep now, young man?"

He nodded.

Emily leaned over and kissed his forehead. "Sweet dreams."

"You, too, Dr. *Señorita*," Marcos said with a sleepy smile and fell back to sleep, as only children can do, the instant he closed his eyes.

Emily sat staring at him. She had just prayed. It was as simple as that — as simple as closing her eyes and talking to someone who loved her. She sighed. Nothing was ever that simple. She rose, straightened his covers, and then turned toward the small connecting room that held his medication and other supplies.

"You're very good with him," Baltasar said, startling her as she entered the room.

Surprised, Emily wondered how long he'd been standing there watching her. "Thank you," she responded and cringed as her voice broke. The last thing she wanted was for him to suspect she'd figured out the truth about him. "He's a special boy." Too special to deserve a drug lord for a father.

His eyes softened, and he dropped onto a stool next to the long blue counter. "He's all I have left in the world that matters to me."

As much as she didn't want to, Emily believed him. She'd had to deal with parents of terminally ill children before. She knew only too well the heartache that lay ahead for him. She wouldn't wish that on her worst enemy. Not even her kidnapper.

"Are the phones up and working yet?" she asked, though she knew it was futile, knew if he had any intention of being aboveboard, he would have asked for her assistance, not demanded it.

"Why do you want to contact the outside world so badly? Are you not happy here? Not treated well? Is the food okay? Your quarters?"

"Yes, everything is fine, that's not the point. There are people at the clinic waiting for Dr. Fletcher and myself, other people, other children, who need us."

"I have talked to Dr. Haynes, the Doctors Without Borders representative, and have assured him that you both are fine, and that you are assisting me with my son on an extremely sensitive issue. He understands completely and has asked me to tell you not to worry about the clinic, things are fine. They have sent for other doctors who will be arriving within the next few days."

"That sounds convenient," she said, the words coming out more bitter than she'd expected.

Baltasar stood. "I love my son and will do whatever I have to do to ensure his last days are comfortable. You can either have a pleasant stay here at my estate, or you can be treated like a prisoner. The choice is entirely yours."

The gloves had just come off.

Emily stiffened and was thankful when he turned and abruptly left the room. She walked into the kitchen and with trembling fingers poured herself a cup of iced tea. As nice as the estate was, she was still a prisoner being held against her will and unable to communicate with anyone. Anyone except for Peter. She had to convince him to help her, and right now was as good a time as any.

She downed her iced tea then made sure Esteban wasn't lurking around before heading out the front door. As soon as she stepped outside an invisible barrier of heat, hot and clinging, hit her. She pushed through it, hugging the side of the house, hoping no one had seen her. She kept to the cobblestone path that led through the tall bushes. Their branches reached for the sky, fighting for the sparse rays of sunlight that made it through the thick canopy of trees.

As she traveled deeper into the grounds, the trees became denser, the sounds more foreign to her. What was she thinking? How could she ever find Peter out here? She didn't even know if he was still at the estate. She would do better to try and find a way to escape on her own. The truth, whether or not she cared to admit it, was that she didn't know who Peter Vance was anymore. He certainly wasn't that long-haired ruffian she'd seen talking about kilos in Baltasar's study.

A loud squawking sounded above her. Her gaze snapped up onto the beady black eyes of a multicolored bird. The raptor-looking thing was more menacing than an object of beauty, with its clawlike beak that could easily tear into her flesh and rip it to shreds. She rubbed her arms. The birds in her travel brochures certainly hadn't looked like this one.

Even the thick tangle of flowering vines appeared to be slowly squeezing the life out of the trees, rather than draping down their trunks like the bridal veils the brochures described. Ha! It was more like suffocation, slow and Machiavellian. She gulped a deep breath, finding it harder and harder to breathe. There was no air here, not even the slightest breeze.

In some places she thought she could see steam rising from the soft earth buried under a thick layer of dead leaves. She grimaced, not even wanting to think about what she could be stepping on. "I'm slowly being cooked alive," she muttered. And, for a second, wondered when she'd veered off the cobblestone path.

A giant insect buzzed past her head. She ducked, then dragged her forearm across her damp forehead. She'd better go back. This wasn't such a good idea. Even if she could find her way off this compound, she'd never find her way out of the jungle. She was trapped.

Something crunched beneath her canvas tennis shoe and her face contorted in disgust. She stared down at the giant cockroaches scurrying around her feet. They were as long as her hand! A hoarse cry erupted from her chest, then caught in her throat and choked her. She turned and ran, unsure of where she was going, just heading back in the direction she'd come, hoping to find her way back to the estate.

She'd been such a fool to come to South America! "An adventure," she muttered. She had seen brochures of incredible beaches, water so blue it made you think you'd found heaven on earth — tropical flowers, waterfalls, beautifully colored birds, paradise on earth.

Paradise? Ha! She was a fool and an idiot. A sharp pain stitched her side, making her stop and double over. "Lord, please help me," she begged, then realized she'd just prayed, again. Twice in one day! A twinge of guilt jabbed her. She stared at the ground waiting for it to open up and swallow her.

She was such a hypocrite, only asking for help when she was desperate and then not living up to her promises, not giving Him the respect He deserved. And this place was her punishment, she thought as she walked down the path carefully watching each strategically placed step. *Perhaps if I ask God to forgive me, if I tried harder to be good. . . .*

Something shifted in the corner of her eye. She stopped and turned, her eyes widening painfully as she stared into the diamond-shaped slits of a hissing reptile. A snake! Not a common garden snake that kids scurry about to catch, but a giant snake with a body the thickness of her thigh. She stood frozen, her heart pounding, unable to move, to scream, to breathe.

Then it began to move. She stood horrified as its sinewy thickness slid up the vine-laden tree beside her. Involuntarily, her mouth snapped open and she gasped a breath of air, allowing the adrenaline to slam into her chest and give her control of her body once more.

Her loud, piercing scream fractured the jungle air, sending flocks of birds fluttering up through the trees and into the sky. Squawking erupted, filling the air, and before she could make her legs move, or let loose another sound, a large, sweaty hand covered her mouth. Her eyes bulged as she was pulled roughly against a hard, masculine chest. A strong arm locked around her waist, lifted her off her feet, and pulled her into the thicket.

She struggled, but it was futile. *Dear Lord, help me.* Peter. Where was Peter? The man stopped moving and dropped her back down onto her feet. He lifted his hand from her face and she could finally draw a deep breath. And she did, lots of them, so many she started to hyperventilate and grow dizzy. She bent over, her hands braced on her knees.

"Stop panicking," the voice snapped.

"Panicking? I'm not panicking. I've passed panicking, I'm bordering on hysterical," she babbled, and then it hit her. She knew this voice. She knew this smell, strong as it was. *She knew this touch.* She swiveled. The beast who had stuck his hot, sweaty palm across her mouth *was* Peter. A haze of red fury seized her, clouding her vision. "Are you out of your mind? What were you thinking grabbing me like that, scaring me half to death?"

"Be quiet!" he demanded.

"No, I won't be quiet. Don't you even tell me to be quiet —"

Once again he picked her up, this time swinging her over his shoulder. The air whooshed out of her lungs and she found she couldn't say another word as he marched off the path and through the bushes.

How dare he? Who did he think he was? And what on earth was wrong with the man? Did he not think she could walk? Something swatted her face. Abruptly she brought up her hands, covering her eyes, not only to protect them from an occasional branch, but also from what she thought she caught sight of scurrying in the bushes. Some things she just didn't want to know about, especially at such close range.

"Ugh!" she groaned as his shoulder dug into her stomach. Her anger intensified and she realized that she was doomed, because there was no way God was going to forgive her for what she was planning on doing to this man once he finally set her down. Before she could contemplate the many ways of primitive medieval torture devices, he unceremoniously plopped her onto the ground.

The blood must have rushed to her head, because she'd barely managed to find her footing, or get a handle on her surroundings through the stars swimming in front of her eyes before he was dragging her in through the back door of a small bungalow.

She opened her mouth to let loose on the cretin, then suddenly the cool air hit her. Abandoning the colorful curses teetering on the tip of her tongue, she immediately rushed to the kitchen sink, turned on the faucet and drowned herself in the icy cold water. Relief. She'd finally found sweet relief, she thought as the water cascaded across her hot sticky skin and rolled around in her mouth.

A rough grip on her shoulder pulled her head out of the sink.

"What did you do that for?" she demanded.

"You were drowning."

"And it felt good, too."

"Suit yourself." He gestured toward the sink.

She promptly stuck her head back under the faucet, relishing the cool water and trying to get hold of her temper. When she finally came up for air, he pushed a towel in her face. "Thank you," she blurted harshly, then kicked off her canvas shoes and promptly deposited them in the trash can under the sink. Then and only then did she turn off the water and turn to face him, the only man she'd ever loved, and the only man she'd ever wanted to do severe harm to.

"Was that little display of Neanderthal He-Manship really necessary or have you been living in this cesspool for too long?"

"You were making too much noise," he said evenly.

"Oh, excuse me for disturbing . . . what? The mutant, diabolical reptiles?"

A smile twitched the corners of his mouth. She raised her fist. "Don't even think about it."

He took a step back, his hand raised in an "I surrender" position. "Don't worry, babe. Wouldn't dream of it."

"Don't call me babe," she growled. "I'm not your babe! I'm not anyone's babe. Got that?" She poked a finger in his chest.

"Okay, okay. No babes, not even a dollface." He leaned against the counter, his face contorting as he visibly tried to get himself under control. Losing the battle, he burst out laughing.

She narrowed her eyes and said the first words that came to her lips. "You are going to have to die."

His bright blue eyes sparkled with laughter, eyes that used to have the ability to turn her to butter. Well, she must be cured of that now; she was sprung way too tight to remotely resemble anything like butter.

"Sorry, love, but I have other plans in mind."

She didn't know whether to pound on his chest in frustration, or throw her arms around his neck and never let go.

"What were you thinking?" she demanded. "You almost gave me a heart attack."

"Was that before or after you just about brought every guard in this place raining down on our heads?"

"Would that have been so bad?"

"Only if Escalante thinks you were trying to escape."

"Well, believe me, any ideas I may have had about that are long gone now."

"Really? Why's that?"

His lips curved and a shiver pulsed through her. She knew what those lips tasted like, and she could almost feel their soft caress and the taste of him rushing through her mouth. She was doomed.

"What are you doing here?" she asked, choosing to ignore him. "Don't you know your family — everyone — has been worried sick about you?" She stared at him and wondered if that could really be her Peter under those long black waves of hair. His vibrant eyes met hers and it was as if time stopped, as if they were the only two people on earth, as if it hadn't been three years since she'd kissed him goodbye in that hospital room and walked out of his life.

"Everyone?" he asked.

She ignored the implication of that raised eyebrow and continued. "And why on earth do you look like that?" She gestured down his body.

"Like what?" he asked with his brown-sugary smooth voice that sent ripples cascading down her throat.

Like incredibly sexy. "Like you're a druggie or something."

"Maybe that's what I am."

She narrowed her eyes and perused his face for obvious signs of drug use: dilated pupils, premature aging and an unfocused, hazy gaze. Nope, his gaze was as sharp as ever. "No way."

"Why not?"

"I know you too well to believe that."

"*Knew* me too well. A lot has happened since I left Colorado."

She sobered as she looked at him. "How have you been, really?" she asked, but what she really wanted to know was, *have you missed me?*

"At this point, better than you."

She had to agree with him on that.

"Baltasar is going to let us go, isn't he?"

Peter took the towel from her hand and draped it over the kitchen chair. "I'm not sure. He's an extremely dangerous man."

"He can't just kidnap and kill two doctors. We're Americans!"

"Somehow, I don't think that fact impresses Baltasar much. You're one of the best pediatric doctors in Colorado. Your specialty happens to be hematology. As long as you're useful to him, you'll be okay. Who arranged for you to come?"

"I did. I talked with Adam — he was down here a few months ago."

"And he was shot by members of a drug cartel. Shouldn't that have given you a clue?"

She drew her lips into a thin line. "Perhaps. We thought we were being careful."

"Obviously not careful enough."

She stiffened. "Fine. We made a mistake. We shouldn't have come. Believe me, we've figured that part out already."

He reached out and touched her hair, pulling a long, wet strand through his fingers. Did he ever think of her? She wanted so badly to tell him she was sorry, to ask him to forgive her, but she couldn't see how that would solve anything. He wasn't the same man she'd left, he was worse. Danger fit him like a well-worn coat, one she could never touch.

"I'd better get back," she said, but couldn't bring herself to move.

He nodded. "Just play it cool. Remember, you don't know me, and whatever you do, stay out of trouble."

She crinkled her forehead into a serious pout. "I don't 'do' trouble."

He smirked. "Yeah, I know." He walked her to the front door and spent a moment looking out the window before letting her leave.

"Peter?"

He turned to her, his face devoid of expression.

"Are you going to get me out of here?" She had to ask, had to know. She tensed waiting for his answer, waiting to see if this time, he'd put her first.

"If I can."

Ah, the big *if.* It wasn't the answer she was hoping for, but at this point she'd take whatever she could get.

"Follow the path back to the main house

as quickly as you can. You don't want to be seen around here."

She nodded.

"And make sure you don't come back. Ever."

His words hurt, but the dead seriousness in his tone scared her more.

"Will I see you again?" she asked in a barely audible whisper.

"Only if you're looking for trouble."

Chapter Four

Peter smiled as Emily walked down the path, her head bent as she focused on each stone before stepping down. His smile faltered though when she stopped to smell a particularly vibrant flower. She certainly didn't look like a woman in fear for her safety. In fact, she appeared to be out for an afternoon stroll. Apparently, he was going to have to go to greater measures to get through to her.

He shook his head as he contemplated how beautiful she still was, and headstrong, and capable of causing him a lot of trouble. He watched until she disappeared from view, then went into the kitchen and pulled her shoes from the garbage can. He spent a few minutes cleaning them up, then placed them in a plastic bag. He couldn't have someone finding them there. He stared at the bag for a moment, wondering what he was going to do with it and supposed he'd have to take them back to her.

He still couldn't believe she was there.

Was it really a coincidence, or did Baltasar know exactly who he was? Had he brought Emily here to use against him? It would be a good plan, for someone calculating and patient. Fortunately, Baltasar was neither of those. With a modicum of relief, Peter decided if the man knew he was an operative, he'd just feed him to his infamous snakes.

In any case, he'd have to be extra careful until Emily was safe on a plane back to Colorado Springs and Vance Memorial because, mission or not, he knew he wouldn't be able to sit back and watch Baltasar torture her. No, he had to get her out of there, whatever the cost. He made sure none of Baltasar's guards were hovering before stealing out his back door and blending into the jungle.

Emily slipped into the courtyard outside the kitchen of the hospital wing and was surprised to find Baltasar and Robert drinking a glass of iced tea together.

"I trust you enjoyed your walk around the grounds?" Baltasar said with a smile that didn't quite reach his eyes.

"I did," Emily said, "until I saw a hideously large snake. Or perhaps it was when I stepped on a cockroach the size of a small rodent." Trying to hide her nervousness, she plastered a look of disgust on her face then stared at her feet.

"For goodness sakes, Emily, where are your shoes?" Robert asked.

Sometimes he was just too paternal. "In the jungle covered in roach guts."

Baltasar laughed.

She looked up in surprise. It was a warm laugh, friendly and genuine. "I hope it was all right to leave, Mr. Escalante, but after our talk this morning, I was feeling a little closed in."

"Of course, it is fine. *Mi casa es su casa.*"

"Thank you," she responded and started for the French doors leading into the house, hoping to get as far away from him as possible.

"And please call me Baltasar," he said with a slight trace of exasperation. "And you don't have to worry, if you see anything that frightens you, all you have to do is call out and one of the guards will assist you immediately. They are always around."

Emily stiffened. Was that a warning? Had there been a guard around earlier? Had she and Peter been seen? "That's good to know," she said and shoved her hands in her pockets to keep them from betraying her anxiety. What if they had been seen? What would that mean, exactly?

"The tall walls keep out the wild boars, the crocs, and a lot of other dangerous animals, but I'm afraid we still have an abundance of snakes and an occasional jaguar."

Emily felt the blood drain from her face.

"Don't worry, Dr. Armstrong, we wouldn't let anything happen to Marcos's favorite doctor." The sharp gleam in his eyes belied his words.

"I'm glad to hear that," she muttered and turned to Robert. "Has Marcos woken from his nap?"

"Not yet."

"Well, then excuse me and I'll go check on him," she said, and hurried through the doors. She could feel Baltasar's eyes on her as she walked into the house. Peter's warning echoed through her mind. But she didn't need the reminder. Of course he's dangerous. Upstanding, rich people didn't kidnap doctors to care for their ailing children, only people who worked outside the law operated that way.

But how dangerous was he? Would he let them go once Marcos died? The thought brought a twinge of sorrow to her heart, but the boy was in the final stages of his illness. She fully expected a stroke to take him at any moment. Once that happened, would Mr. Escalante just open up the gates and bid them farewell or would an unfortunate accident befall the two doctors from America? No one would know any better. No one but Peter. She squeezed her eyes shut and hoped she was wrong.

As she approached Marcos's room, she heard the faint sounds of crying. She hurried forward. "Marcos, what is it? What's wrong?" she asked as she entered the door.

"It hurts, Dr. *Señorita.*"

"Where, show me?"

"Here." He pointed to his lungs, then added, "Everywhere."

She checked his chart to see what type of medication he'd already been given, then opened a drawer and took out a new hypodermic needle and proceeded to squeeze a dose of morphine into his intravenous line. She held his small hand and gave it a light squeeze. "There, just give it a minute to kick in and you'll feel better."

How she hated to see children wracked with pain. Sometimes she wasn't sure why she put herself through it. To help, she thought. All she wanted to do was help and try to find a way to fix it, to make it better. Sometimes she almost succeeded. Unfortunately, this wouldn't be one of those times. Marcos's condition couldn't be fixed.

Tears leaked out the corners of his eyes as waves of pain rolled through his little body. She held tight to his hand, not only to assure him that she was there, but to keep her emotions in check. The tears flowed freely down his cheeks as he battled with his pain. Trying to distract him, she started to sing. "Once there was a silly old ant. . . ."

As the song ended, he opened his eyes, met her gaze and held it for a long moment. "Am I going to die, Dr. *Señorita?*"

The honesty of his question shining through eyes too wise for his eight years touched her with a gentle stroke of sadness. "You're a very sick little boy, Marcos. I won't lie to you about that."

Silently he stared at her, willing her to continue, willing her to tell him he was going to be all right, that he'd be able to go to school like other children and grow up to drive a car, to live. She swallowed. She couldn't do it. Instead, she asked, "Did you know that your mama is with you every moment of the day? Watching over you, helping you?"

He nodded. "And Jesus, too. My mama told me Jesus would never leave me. No matter what we do, He will always be there for us. He loves us."

"How did you get to be such a smart little man?"

"I was just born that way."

She smiled. The stark paleness to his skin began to lift and his face filled with color. The medicine was finally working. "Are you feeling better?"

He nodded and his eyelids grew heavy.

She watched him for a long moment.

"Dr. *Señorita*, what was that song you were singing?"

"It's a song about a little ant that has high hopes. Did you like it?"

He nodded. "Will you sing it to me again?"

She brushed the hair back from his forehead and sang softly as he drifted to sleep.

A few minutes later Baltasar walked in. He watched his son sleeping, then turned his attention to her. "How is he doing?"

"Honestly?"

"Please."

She got up and led him into the kitchen, not wanting Marcos to wake and overhear them. "I had to give him morphine tonight. The pain is beginning to overwhelm him."

Anguish flashed in his eyes. Right then,

he wasn't a monster, but a father about to lose his son. She placed a hand on his arm. "I'm sorry, but for the next few days you should spend as much time with him as you possibly can."

"His mother went the same way."

"She had HIV?"

"It was bad. Heartbreaking. I thought at the time it was the hardest thing I'd ever have to live through. Now I know different."

"I'm sorry. He's a wonderful little boy. Unfortunately, all I'm going to be able to do is make him as comfortable and pain-free as I can."

"I'm not expecting anything more."

She nodded and turned to go.

"Dr. Armstrong, will you join me for dinner?"

Emily hesitated. She knew he wanted to talk, to try and work through what he was about to face, but she didn't think she was up to pretending she wasn't afraid of him through an entire dinner.

"Please, it's the least I can do."

Before she could answer, Robert walked into the room and poured himself a cup of coffee. "Robert, have you eaten?" she asked and hoped he'd be able to join them. At least then she could focus on him and not on wondering whether or not Baltasar was going to let them go home, or if they'd suffer the same fate as Marcos's last doctor.

"I just finished. My compliments to the chef, Mr. Escalante."

"Baltasar, please. I know it seems like you're prisoners here, but I want you to feel like my guests. In fact, I've already made a rather substantial contribution to the Doctors Without Borders clinic as compensation for the time you are spending here."

"That was very generous," Robert said with a touch of sincerity in his tone, but there was a stiffness to his back, a hardness to his jaw, and Emily knew he was just as concerned as she was.

"Ready?" Baltasar asked.

With one last look at Robert, she nodded, then followed Baltasar down the hall.

Peter sat for a long time watching the sun dip lower in the sky, wondering how he was going to be able to keep Emily safe without jeopardizing his mission. His cover as Pietro Presti had to stay in place. One slipup and they were all dead. And in the jungle, death could be nasty.

He took out his phone and made an un-scheduled call. It took several rings before he knew his father, Max, would be able to find a secure location to answer.

"This better be good," his father growled.

"Baltasar wants a test," he said getting right to the point.

He heard paper rustling on the other end before his father said, "Okay, shoot."

"A mule, female named Melinda Rodriguez, will be arriving at the Thurston hotel in Chicago for a drop at noon tomorrow. At the same time, three more women named Melinda Rodriguez will be arriving at the Williams, Barston and Executor — all along the river, all at the same time. I need couriers available in each hotel to make the pickups."

"Got it. This is good. Great work."

"I have an unexpected problem." He heard his dad take a deep breath and hesi-tated, not exactly sure how to break the news. He opted for short and sweet. "Emily's here."

Max blew out a profanity.

"Mom will get you for that," Peter said, and felt a pang of homesickness. He missed his mother's laugh, her smile, her good Italian home cooking.

"I knew there'd be a problem the minute

I heard she and Robert were heading down there, but I couldn't do a thing about it. What is she doing there? Why isn't she at the clinic?"

"Apparently Baltasar intercepted them at the airport and brought them here to care for his son. I can't leave her here alone on the night of the raid."

"Baltasar will be with you. Instruct her to head for the clinic as soon as you've gone."

"I can't. I don't even want to think about what his goons might do to her if anything goes wrong."

"I'll work on it on this end and see what we can come up with. But I'm warning you, son, you need to stay away from her and stay focused on your assignment. For both your sakes."

Unfortunately, Peter knew his father was right. Before disconnecting, Max gave him the coordinates for the drug processing lab along the Colombian border. In another week, the renegade air force pilots working for General Hadley were expected to bring Baltasar his money and pick up another five hundred kilos destined for Colorado. Only there wouldn't be one penny of drug money on that plane; instead it would be full of CIA, DEA and FBI operatives. He would be at the lab when the raid went down, but first he had to figure out what to do with Emily.

He pocketed the phone and walked toward the main house, checking it from one end to the other. Luckily, Baltasar had his guards on a standard rotation schedule that didn't seem to vary much. He checked once again to make sure his timing was right, then approached the hospital wing. Emily wasn't there. He found Dr. Fletcher dozing in a chair in front of a large-screen TV, but no sign of Emily.

He slipped back out the door and into the courtyard, glancing through as many windows as he could as he followed the courtyard behind the back of the house, through the pool area and cabanas where two guards were smoking cigarettes and cursing in Spanish as they played pool.

From what he could decipher, one of the guards wasn't too happy with Emily and wanted to teach her a lesson. Peter's fists clenched as he listened to the guard rant and rave. He was beginning to believe it would take a miracle for Emily to get out of this country unscathed.

Silently, he slipped through the tall bushes and trees that outlined the house. He stopped next to Baltasar's study. The room was dark and empty. Now would be the perfect time to slip in and search his desk and computer files, but the persistent thought that Emily could be in danger kept nagging at him. Lord only knew what kind of trouble she'd gotten herself into now. It was always something. That impulsive streak of hers was going to be their down-fall, he just knew it.

Reluctantly, he passed by Baltasar's office and kept circling around the building, all the while hoping she hadn't been foolish enough to go out into the jungle at night alone. Although he knew if she'd gotten it into her mind that would solve her problems, then he had no doubt that was exactly what she'd do.

As he continued his surveillance, he heard her laughter chiming through the night carried on the balmy air. He hurried forward, drawn as much by the sound as he was by his need to see her, to prove to himself that she was okay and still in the house.

He turned a corner and suddenly stopped as the acrid scent of tobacco smoke hit him. He wasn't alone. He moved cautiously forward until he spotted a soft red glow through the thick green leaves. Careful not to make a sound, he crept closer. He heard Emily's laugh again and saw her clearly through the window. Who would be standing in the bushes, spying on Emily?

Snake.

Like death's heavy black cloak, dread settled over Peter as he watched Baltasar's number one henchman stand concealed in the bushes spying on Baltasar and Emily. He tried to determine what could be so interesting about them having dinner. They were sitting at the end of an enormous dining table, talking like old friends, laughing, having an all-around good time. Peter's gut clenched. Hadn't he warned her? Hadn't he told her how dangerous Baltasar could be? And there she was doing what she'd always done, doing whatever she pleased.

He fumed as he watched Baltasar grow more and more enamored with his wife. Correction — his *ex*-wife and with good reason, too. The woman refused to listen. Snake dropped his cigarette and ground it into the soft earth. Who was he interested in, Emily or Baltasar? Peter watched as Snake disappeared around the front of the house. The man would bear closer watching.

Satisfied that Emily was indeed safe,

Peter left the main house to check the other bungalows and try to exact a head count of how many guards were at the compound and when they patrolled and where. Two hours later, he made his way back to the dining room. He was more than a little relieved to find it empty. He headed toward Baltasar's office; unfortunately, the drug lord was there pounding away on his computer. Peter would have to check back later for another opportunity to search Baltasar's office.

He continued around back, past the pool and the guards in the cabana and into the courtyard off the hospital wing. The television was turned off and the room was dark; Robert must have called it a night. Peter slipped in and locked the door behind him, even though he was certain the guards probably all had keys. The thought bothered him, but he didn't see any way around it.

He continued down the hall to Emily's room, and peeked through her door. The tension dropped out of his shoulders at the sight of her sleeping peacefully in her bed. He crept into her room and stood over her for a moment, looking down at her blond hair fanning the pillow. Shafts of moonlight spilled across her face. He stared at her, amazed that she still had the ability to take his breath away.

A soft breeze blew in through the open window and he was tempted to sit in the chair next to her bed and watch her sleep. But he couldn't. He still had a long night ahead of him surveilling the compound and gathering as much information as he could. She moaned slightly, her lips parting as she let out a gentle sigh and before he could stop himself, he lightly grazed his thumb across her lips. He wished he could lean down and take a small taste, but while she could play the role of Sleeping Beauty, he was no Prince Charming.

He forced himself to walk away.

"Don't go," she said softly.

He stopped, stiffening. "I didn't mean to wake you."

"Why are you here?"

"I needed to check for myself that you're okay." No, that wasn't true. He knew she was okay, he just wanted to be near her again, to see if all those feelings he'd been carrying around were still for her, or for what used to be.

She sat up. "I'm okay . . . now that you're here."

He ignored the breathiness in her tone,

the implications of her words, and the un-spoken invitation in the way the blanket fell down to hover at her waist, revealing a modest pale pink nightgown that shone in the soft light of the moon. "I should go," he said, before he did something he couldn't take back.

"There's so much . . . I've wished we could say."

"We don't need to rehash everything again." There was no reason. Nothing had changed.

She looked down at her lap and fiddled with the covers.

"Have you found anyone . . . ?" It was awkward. He didn't know why he asked. It was none of his business, and yet, all this time the only way he'd been able to make it through the long nights was by con-vincing himself that she'd moved on, that she was happy in a way he would never be able to make her. If he knew for sure, then maybe he'd be able to move on, too, and fi-nally find some peace.

"No," she said softly.

It was amazing how that one word, with its one simple syllable could have such an impact on his gut. He took a deep breath. "Why not? You should have married by now, you should be raising babies. Isn't that what you've always wanted?" *Isn't that why we're not together?* The unspoken words burned inside him.

"I guess I'm a tough case — too hard to please."

Her words were vague, but her eyes said so much more. She hadn't gotten over him, either. "Don't say that," he whispered.

"It's true."

"Emily. We can't go back. Things are different now —"

"I know. Things are even worse. If you weren't courting danger before . . . you're sleeping with it now."

"I'm sorry. That's my life."

Her eyes shone bright in the moonlight. "Why are you here, Peter?"

"I can't tell you." He wished he could. Maybe it would make a difference, maybe it would make her more careful, and maybe it would get her killed.

She stood and faced him. "Of course. You never could tell me anything about your work. Maybe if you had, I wouldn't have felt so alone, so isolated."

He raked a hand through his hair. This was getting them nowhere. "I thought we weren't going to go down that road again."

"All right, but just tell me one thing."

"If I can."

"Are you selling drugs? Or —"

Peter stiffened. "Like I said, I can't talk about my work."

Her lips started to tremble and she looked at him with such heartbreak on her face, he felt an overwhelming urge to pull her into his arms and assure her that everything would be all right, but he knew it wouldn't be all right. Not for them, not ever again.

"All I can tell you is that Baltasar is dangerous. Be careful around him and especially around his guards. I'll try to get you out as soon as I can." He had to.

She nodded. "Then will you be coming back home?"

"Nothing has changed, Emily. There isn't anything left in Colorado Springs for me." It was harsh, but it had to be said. He couldn't leave her with any false illusions. Nothing had changed. He was still the same man he was three years ago when she'd walked out of his hospital room and divorced him.

"A lot has changed," she said, and wrapped her arms around his neck and pulled his head down.

Before he could stop it, his lips met hers in a fiery explosion that he couldn't resist. She felt exactly as he knew she would:

sweet, luscious, seductive. More tempta-
tion than he could withstand. His blood
thickened as their kiss deepened. He
pulled her closer and grabbed fistfuls of
her silky hair. How he missed her, he
thought, with a longing that ached more
than he could bear.

No, he had to stop this. It was only going
to make things worse and put them in
greater danger. "Emily," he breathed and
pulled back. "I want —" he opened his
eyes and saw a small red glow burn bright
outside her window. *Snake.* His heart
slammed into the side of his chest. He
pushed her away then ran to the open
window. Snake was gone, but the distinc-
tive scent of his cigarettes still wafted in
the air.

"Peter, what is it?"

How long had Snake been standing
there, watching . . . listening? A silent
dread moved steadily through him. How
much had he heard?

Chapter Five

Confusion filled Emily as she watched Peter at the window. "Peter, what is it?" Her mind, still reeling from their kiss, couldn't grasp what was wrong. It didn't help that her lips were still tingling, her heart still aching.

"Emily, you have to leave. Now." He grabbed her duffel bag out of the closet and started throwing her stuff in it.

He wanted her to go that badly? Just because of one little kiss? Okay, one great kiss, but still. "Don't be ridiculous, Peter. We're in the middle of the jungle. I've been out there during the day, and I can guarantee you there is no way I'm going out there at night."

"He saw us."

"Who?"

"Snake."

"Oh." Just the sound of his name sent a quiver rushing down her spine. "So, he saw us kiss. Aren't people allowed to kiss in South America?"

"He could have heard us."

She didn't like his quick, jerky movements, or the way his jaw looked as if he were biting down on his teeth, trying to keep himself calm. She'd never seen him look that way before. Ever.

"He'll know we were married. He'll know I used to live in Colorado Springs. He could have heard you call me Peter," he rasped.

Emily's knees weakened. "You are still with the CIA. I knew it! You're working undercover trying to stop the drug trade —"

"Keep out of it, Emily."

"I can't keep out of it. Like you said, Snake saw us kissing. Lord, they're going to kill you."

Peter muttered a curse and paced back and forth across the room. "No one is going to get killed. Not you and certainly not me."

She put her hand on his arm, stopping him. "You'll get us out of this. I know you will, because you're good at what you do. When the time comes, you'll know exactly what to say and do."

He speared his fingers through his hair. "I have to find a way to get you out of here."

"Peter, stop it." She caught her breath as he turned to her. She'd never seen him look so worried, so scared. "You're focusing on me and I'm not the one in danger right now. Baltasar needs me to care for his son, and nothing is going to happen to me as long as he does. Now, remove me from the equation and think about what you would do if I wasn't here."

Peter took a deep breath and nodded. "You're right. Worrying about you is definitely interfering with my ability to concentrate."

"That's nice to hear." She smiled, leaned forward and kissed him lightly on the lips.

He brought his hands to her cheeks and pulled her forward, kissing her hard and deep, and leaving her breathless. He came up for air. "We need a plan."

Marcos groaned from the other room. Emily pulled away. "I have to go to him."

"All right, but don't leave the hospital wing. I'm going to find Snake and try to determine what he saw and heard."

"Okay, be careful," she said as fear for his safety flooded through her, making it difficult to think.

"Meet me tomorrow morning at eight o'clock where I found you today."

"By that giant snake?"

Peter opened the screen and swung his legs out the window. "Better get used to

the snakes, baby, the jungle's full of them."
He stepped into the bushes and disappeared.

Emily didn't like the way the jungle swallowed him whole. She shut the screen and closed the window, unnervingly aware of how easy it would be for someone to watch her. She hurried as the sound of another groan reached her. Why hadn't she stayed home in her nice, safe little apartment in her idyllic American town? "Because I wanted a little adventure, a little excitement," she muttered. "And I sure got it — aren't I lucky?"

Peter spotted Snake's trail and retraced his steps before they disappeared into the thick grass. He continued around the house and found Snake in Baltasar's office. Peter moved in as close as he dared outside the office window and hoped Snake wouldn't give away what he'd seen and heard.

"Is everything as we expect?" Baltasar asked.

Peter's heart raced as he waited for Snake to speak.

Snake nodded, and leaned forward, mumbling something Peter couldn't quite catch.

Frustration mounted inside him as Baltasar tipped back his chair. "I want preparations made. Nothing can go wrong." He picked up the phone. After a few seconds, he said, "I want the drop point changed for the shipment."

Peter moved forward, suddenly aware that they weren't talking about him and Emily but about the upcoming shipment of cash he was expecting.

"I can't get a hold of Barclay," Baltasar barked into the phone. "Get hold of General Hadley. Make sure nothing holds up this shipment. I won't leave Marcos. I want the plane to come in here instead of the lab. Yes, here at the compound. And I want it earlier than we scheduled. Find Hadley and make it happen." Baltasar nodded and chuckled. "And if you do see Barclay, issue an invitation to the weasel. I want him to come to South America and meet Leona. I don't like the way he's been handling my interests lately. His obsession with his bid for mayor is interfering with him running Diablo properly."

Peter wondered who Baltasar was talking to. Who would be in position in Colorado Springs to get to Hadley and change the drop? Obviously, there was another of Baltasar's cohorts they weren't aware of, and if he discovered the CIA has Barclay, then their whole operation would be shot.

He had to get ahold of his father.

He turned to leave, then stopped when he heard Baltasar bellow, "Pietro and Dr. Armstrong? Are you sure?"

Peter glanced back into the study, his gut twisting with dread.

"I don't like this, Snake. I have too much riding on this deal for some lowlife pig to screw it up for me now."

Snake nodded, but didn't speak loud enough for Peter to hear what he said.

"I will wait to hear from my operatives in Chicago tomorrow. Once the product is transferred, Pietro and I will have a little talk. Apparently, he needs a lesson in boundaries."

Peter heaved a sigh of relief. He had a short reprieve. The Chicago shipment would go down at noon tomorrow — that meant he had until one o'clock to get the information he needed on Baltasar's man in Colorado. If the CIA messed up the pickup at the hotels, he'd be out on his ear, if he was lucky. The noose clinched his neck and Peter couldn't say he liked the fit.

"This doctor has been trouble from the start. I want a full background check done on Dr. Armstrong, more detailed than what you did last time. Go beyond her time at Vance Memorial. I want to know everything. Got it?"

Snake nodded and rose.

Peter ducked back out of sight, and wondered how long it would take Snake to get a picture of Emily and him on their wedding day. The noose squeezed tighter.

"We've got a problem," Peter whispered into his phone once he reached his bungalow.

"What now?" Max asked.

"Baltasar wants the location of the drop changed to the estate."

Maxwell Vance let loose a heavy sigh. "What on earth for? The risk is too high. The Venezuelan authorities monitor air traffic that close to Caracas."

"He won't leave his son. He must have arranged a payoff. He also wants the date of the drop moved up."

Max muttered a curse so loud and so vile Peter's ears burned.

"Apparently he still has a contact working for him in Colorado Springs. He told him to get ahold of Hadley and make the changes."

There was a moment of silence. "All right, we'll spring Hadley and make it happen. Then maybe we'll even be able to flush out who this guy is."

"Also, tell Barclay that Baltasar wants him to meet Leona. That might loosen his lips."

"Who's Leona?"

"I don't know. But it didn't sound like a friendly meeting." Peter took a second, then said the words he'd been dreading. "Dad, my cover's been compromised." Anxiety burned in Peter's chest. He hated to let his father down, but worse, he couldn't quite stomach the fact that he might fail a mission.

"What happened?" his father asked softly.

"Emily."

"Is she in danger?"

"Even more so now."

"All right. Get her out of there and keep a low profile."

"I don't have time to take her myself. I need to make sure I'm here at one when the deal goes down in Chicago."

"Then get her to go on her own. Nothing can happen to her, understand. She's . . . family."

Peter closed his eyes and sucked in a breath. "I know, Dad. Is everything in line in Chicago? That deal going down exactly right could be the only thing that saves this situation."

"It will go down like clockwork."

Peter sighed. "At least something is working the way it should."

"You can salvage this, Peter. I know you can."

"Maybe, if I didn't have Emily to worry about. Baltasar ordered a full background check."

"Get her off that mountain. That's an order."

"Whatever it takes, Dad."

"Go careful out there, son, and make sure you come home in one piece."

The next morning, Emily lay in bed and stared at the ceiling. She wasn't sure she wanted to face what the day could bring — Marcos growing sicker, Snake and Esteban constantly lurking about, and Peter . . . Her mind was well aware of the danger he was facing, the danger he still continued to face on a daily basis. Yet her heart couldn't forget the way she'd felt when he looked at her, touched her. She still fit neatly into his arms. And his kiss . . . she sighed as a long ache moved through her.

She wanted him back.

She stared at the plump pillow next to her and wished he were there, but he'd left her alone. With Peter she would always be waiting for him to come home, always wondering if he would. Frustrated with her thoughts, she got out of bed and showered. Dwelling on the past would get her nowhere. It was the future she needed to think about and how they were going to get themselves out of South America.

She plastered a smile on her face and walked into Marcos's room. For the time being she needed to focus on the boy and not worry about Peter until she saw him again and found out how much danger they were actually in. "Hey there, little man, how are you feeling this morning?" She noticed his breakfast tray still sitting in front of him. "Is something wrong with your food?"

Marcos looked down at his tray, his bottom lip protruding. "No."

"You need to eat more to keep up your strength."

He looked up at her. "I know, Dr. *Señorita.* I'm just not hungry this morning. My stomach is not good."

Emily nodded, understanding. "Then let's get you something different to eat." She picked up the plate of eggs and bacon and walked into the other room. Her heart lurched as she saw Esteban leaning against the wall, leering at her. She squared her shoulders, then thrust the plate into his grasp. "Can you take this back to the kitchen and have the chef make Marcos some hot cereal? Tell him something easy on his stomach."

Esteban stared at the plate in his hand, then stuck a piece of the bacon in his mouth, and left the room without saying a word. If she was lucky, she could disappear to meet up with Peter before he made it back with the cereal.

She hurried back into Marcos's room and froze when she saw Baltasar sitting next to his bed. She shook off her alarm and forced herself to look normal, casual, to look like she wasn't facing a man who could snuff out her life with the snap of his fingers.

"Good morning, Dr. Armstrong," Baltasar greeted.

"Good morning," she responded. She smiled, and searched his expression for any sign that he knew about Peter, about them, but she didn't see anything different in his face. Perhaps they'd been worrying about nothing. She hoped so.

"I sent Esteban to the kitchen to get Marcos some hot cereal. His stomach is a little queasy this morning."

"Thank you, that was very thoughtful."

"We all want Marcos to feel better." She

turned to her patient. "After you eat your cereal and rest, how about if you and I take a walk in the gardens?"

"I can?" He turned to his father.

"I think the fresh air will do him good," Emily added, and fiddled with his monitors to make sure everything was operating properly and to keep her hands from fluttering with nervousness.

"If the doctor thinks it will be good for you, then absolutely you should get some fresh air," Baltasar said. "In fact, I will join you, *bien?*"

"You're on," Marcos said with more animation than he'd shown a few minutes before.

"I'll see you at ten, then?" Baltasar asked, and pierced her with one of his cold gazes.

Emily nodded, so much for keeping away from Baltasar and his men. At least she would still have a little time with Peter. If he was where he said he'd be. After Baltasar left, she waited a few minutes for him to make it back to his side of the estate, then gave Marcos's shoulder a squeeze. "Your cereal should be here any minute. I'm going out for a quick walk, but I'll be back soon. If you need anything, ring for nurse Marguerite or Dr. Fletcher, *bien?*"

He gave her a small smile, then held up the remote and clicked on the television. "All right, Dr. *Señorita.*"

She slipped out the door before Esteban arrived with the cereal and retraced her steps from the day before. Why Peter couldn't have met her in his cool and comfortable bungalow, she couldn't fathom. They could be alone there. Maybe he didn't want to be alone, she thought.

The doubts ate at her as she made her way across the compound. Maybe he didn't feel the same way she did. No. He was trying to resist her, too — she felt it in his touch and saw it in the way he looked at her. He couldn't hide his feelings for her any more than she could hide hers from him. His kiss gave him away.

As she moved deeper into the jungle, she slowed on the path, listening for Peter or anything else that might be out there lurking. She was careful to watch where she stepped, but couldn't help but be overwhelmed by the multitude of large insects. It was so hot she could barely breathe and sweat was dripping down her back. Suddenly, she stopped. Sitting in the middle of an incredibly intricate web was a spider as big as her fist.

Her heart jumped into her throat and

her nerves danced a jig up and down her spine. Before she could turn away, someone covered her eyes, blinding her. She took a deep breath, ready to roar with frustration, afraid more than anything to lose sight of that humongous arachnid.

"Shh, it's only me," Peter whispered.

"I know it's only you. Get your hands off me," she demanded.

He removed his hands and stepped back.

Luckily, the spider was still hanging in the center of its web. She whirled on him. "Why can't you ever approach me like a rational, sane human being?"

"What, and miss the fun of seeing you all flushed and angry?"

"You really are too much."

"Yep, way too much for you to handle."

"Oh yeah?" she challenged and was tempted to lean forward and kiss that smug look right off his face. Then he'd see exactly how much she could handle. Instead she stepped to the other side of the path, keeping the spider in her field of vision. "What did you want?"

"I need to show you something."

She wasn't sure she could take anymore. "Tell me it's close by. There's no way I'm moving any farther into this jungle."

"It's not so bad, once you learn to respect it."

She looked at the huge, hairy spider and realized she did respect it. A lot. That didn't mean she wanted to be around it or even know it existed.

He took her hand and led her farther down the path. "The guards pass this way every thirty minutes. Move through here." He pointed between two large bushes.

"But that's off the cobblestone path," she protested as the image of what happened the last time she veered off the path flashed through her mind. She wasn't anxious for a repeat visit with any snakes or giant cockroaches. "Besides, there are spiderwebs everywhere."

"It's okay. Trust me." As he said the word, something in his eyes touched her heart. He'd said those words to her before, when they'd been happy and married, and she'd been so afraid he'd get hurt. *I'm careful. Nothing will happen. Trust me.* And she had. But he'd been wrong, something did happen.

She shook off the painful memories and silently followed him through the bushes, keeping her eyes alert for large, slithering, crawly things in front of her and icky, crunchy things beneath her feet. "I don't know how you can ever get used to this," she muttered as she awkwardly made her way through the bushes.

Peter glanced back over his shoulder and smiled. "All this stuff just keeps you on your toes."

"To say the least. No leisurely strolls back here."

"Don't let yourself be fooled by the manicured grounds by the house. There are a lot more dangerous things to worry about around here than snakes and spiders."

"Like Baltasar?"

"Exactly."

"Is he a drug lord?"

Peter didn't respond but stopped in front of the high block wall. He pulled back a blooming vine and revealed a rope ladder. "On the other side of this wall, I've stashed a motorcycle. I want you to take it and go back to Caracas and catch the next flight home."

Disbelief filled her as she stared at him. "You're not serious?"

"Deadly."

"You want me to climb this monstrous wall? I'd kill myself when I dropped down on the other side."

"It's not that far."

"I don't even know how to start a motor-cycle, let alone ride one. Then I'm supposed to make my way off this mountain through the jungle without getting lost. All by myself. Are you nuts?" she shrieked.

"You can manage. I have faith in you."

"Gee, thanks. That makes me feel so much better."

"I'm serious, Emily. I know it will be hard, but you can do it. What you can't do is stay here. It's too dangerous."

"Somehow I think it's a lot safer on this side of the wall than on that." As she gestured toward the wall, she remembered Baltasar's warning about crocodiles, wild boars and jaguars. "Forget it. There's no way."

"This is your life we're talking about."

"You can protect me. I have faith in *you*," she said, turning his words back on him.

He hesitated, his eyes narrowing. "I can't protect you and do my job."

Ah, the real dilemma. Get rid of her so he can focus on what really matters, what really counts — his job. Pain stiffened her spine. "I won't leave without Robert."

"Fine, I'll bring him to you. Climb the ladder and wait on the other side of the wall. You can both fit on the bike."

"Peter, I won't go into that jungle. I'd

never find my way back to Caracas. I'm not leaving."

"You can see the ocean from the other side of the wall. Just head toward the sea, then once you get on a main road, follow the signs. You'll make it."

"I won't. I can't even believe you're asking me to do this. The Peter I knew would never try and push me to do something I didn't want to."

"Or force you to stay if you didn't want to."

"What?" She stared at him. Is that why he let her go? Understanding brought a bitter pang of regret.

Emotion flashed in his eyes: pain, disappointment, anger . . .

"I shouldn't have kissed you last night. Snake saw us and he told Baltasar. It's only a matter of time before he finds out we were married and that I'm not Pietro Presti from Chicago. When that happens, I won't be able to protect you."

She was silent for a moment, absorbing everything he said and everything he didn't. There was a lot more at stake here than his job. This mission could very well get him killed. Sorrow filled her. "I kissed you," she said softly.

"What?"

"You didn't kiss me, *I* kissed *you*."

"What difference does that make?"

"A lot. It means I'm sorry. It means I care. It means I miss you and I don't want to go down that mountain unless you come with me." She stepped forward. "I don't want to leave you." *Please come with me.*

"You already left me, Emily, years ago. There's no turning back. Not now, not ever."

"You still care, I know you do."

"That's not the point."

"Then what is? What else matters?"

"I can't trust you not to change your mind again and decide you can't live with the uncertainty that goes with my job."

"That's hardly fair."

"Isn't it?"

"I'm not some silly schoolgirl who doesn't know my heart."

"Really. Then you're okay with my job, that it's dangerous and sometimes you might not hear from me. You might not know where I am and what I'm doing."

She bit her lip as the truth of his words hit her. She did care, that was the problem. "Why can't you give it up?"

"For what?"

"For me?"

He stared at her. "Because it wouldn't

be enough, you'd always want more and I'd keep giving until there was nothing left of me. Can't you see that?"

Frustrated tears shimmered in her eyes. "No, all I can see is that you could possibly die and you'd rather face death than love me enough to try and make it work between us."

"Em, climb the ladder." Once more he pulled back the vine. "Go home and forget you ever saw me here."

"No, Peter. I won't forget. If you want me safe, you're going to have to come with me. I won't leave you. Not again."

Chapter Six

Emily couldn't spend another moment looking into Peter's eyes, seeing the pain, the mistrust, the broken dreams. And she'd caused it all, because she had been too afraid. She'd let fear take over her life and she pushed him away, and now he was doing the same thing. He was afraid so he was pushing her away. No matter how she felt, no matter what the risk. He just wanted her to go home and forget she ever saw him, forget they ever kissed.

That may be easier for him, but for her it would be impossible. Tears filled her eyes. "Sorry, Peter, but I can't go." She turned and ran back the way she'd come straight into the jungle, searching for the blasted cobblestone path, swatting at the tears running down her cheeks. She'd been such a fool. She'd bared her soul, laid her feelings on the line and he'd taken her heart and stomped on it. *Forget.*

She wasn't a child, a selfish little girl who takes and takes. She respected him for who he was, she just preferred to have a husband who was actually living. Why couldn't he see that? Why couldn't he see that she just wanted what she knew they could have together?

As a sharp stitch threaded her side she stopped running and looked around her. She was completely and hopelessly lost. She started walking, slowly this time, listening for any sound from Baltasar's guards. She couldn't believe it, but she was actually hoping to run into one of them. She skirted another massive web, and shuddered when she couldn't see its host. Better the guards than anything else she could think of.

Even Peter? The silent question mocked her, sending a tender ache spreading through her. Emotion clogged her throat. She pushed it back down. She wouldn't think about him, about everything they'd once had and lost, about everything they would never have again because he wouldn't let them have it again. He'd rather live alone in this horrid dark green nightmare of a jungle than come home with her. Somehow, she had to find a way to change his mind.

Sweat ran down her back, and her legs itched. In her rush out the door, she'd forgotten to put on her bug spray and was beginning to pay the consequences for her lapse in active brain cells — an affliction that seemed to be growing. Thank goodness she hadn't listened to Peter and climbed that wall.

She brushed another disgusting insect off her thigh, then heard a rustling in the bushes to her right. She stopped and forced herself to breathe. She scanned the leaves and branches, but saw nothing. She expelled a breath then let her gaze roam to the nearest tree where it crashed head on with the sharp yellow-green eyes of a black jaguar.

Her heart jumped painfully into her throat as little mewling sounds escaped her. She couldn't move, couldn't think. How was it possible that this monster cat could just be sitting there this close to the house . . . on this side of that wall?

She stood frozen, waiting for him to rip her to shreds. "Help," she squeaked through her closed throat. The cat's eyes bored into hers, its whiskers twitched. "Help," she called again, a little louder this time. Gracefully, it stood up on the large limb and moved toward her. It would only be mere seconds before it pounced.

Don't run, she told herself. *It'll chase you down and eat you.* And even though she knew it was a mistake, she couldn't help herself. She wanted to run. She needed to run. She shifted her weight.

"Dr. Armstrong?" Baltasar said, walking up behind her and nearly giving her a heart attack.

"Shh," she said, and without turning to look, reached one hand behind her to stop him from approaching. Afraid to take her eyes off the beast, she said, "Back up slowly."

"I see you've met Akisha."

Horrified confusion coursed through her. "Akisha?" This time she did turn. She couldn't have heard him right. "You've named it?"

Baltasar smiled at her, but it wasn't a friendly smile, it was cold, ruthless and predatory.

Oh, no! It was his pet. His killing machine. He was going to feed her to his cat, just like he probably fed the last doctor to his monster pet snakes. Oh, Peter was right! She was going to die. She should have gone over the stupid wall.

"What are you doing out here?" he asked.

She grabbed hold of her rising panic and reined it in. "I got lost," she said, flushing. She couldn't breathe. The heat was overwhelming, her head was swimming, and to make her situation even worse, even more desperate, she thought she felt something tickling her ankle. She lifted her foot and prayed for balance. "I don't think I feel well, Mr. Escalante."

"You don't look well. Our jungle atmosphere must be too much for you. Perhaps you should stick closer to the house."

Emily nodded. "I think you're right."

"This is a little far off the beaten path for you to just get lost." His words were casual, but his stance was stiff and wary.

"I was just taking a little walk," she said, trying to explain herself and remove the suspicion from his face. "But I walked into this giant spiderweb and just about died when I saw what was sitting in it and, well . . . I'm afraid I got spooked and I ran, but I must have gone in the wrong direction because suddenly I'm standing here about to become this cat's breakfast."

He didn't laugh, didn't even crack a smile. Instead, he said, "Don't worry about Akisha. She's already eaten."

Emily looked back at the cat. Eaten or not, she was sure it would have taken immense pleasure in batting her around a bit and perhaps pulling off an arm or two. "I wish I could say I find that comforting."

"Esteban!" Baltasar called, turning behind him.

Esteban stepped out of the bushes."

"Sí, señor?"

Emily stiffened at the sight of the small guard. How was it he always seemed to appear out of nowhere? Had he been following her? Had he seen her with Peter?

"Please see the doctor makes it back to the house." He placed a guiding hand on her shoulder, forcing her toward the guard. "I'm sure Marcos will be waking soon and will want to go on that walk through the gardens. I'll meet you back there in an hour."

She nodded, and couldn't help noticing that he didn't order Esteban to get her back to the house *safely*. Perhaps Peter was right, perhaps her time was running out.

Peter stood far back in the bushes and watched the exchange. He held his breath, wondering what Baltasar would do next. Would he feed her to his favorite pet? His insides burned as the cruel smile came over his nemesis's face. Baltasar was on to her; it was only a matter of time before he'd turn on her.

Why couldn't he have convinced her to

leave? Never had he met a more frustrating, impulsive and headstrong woman. How had he ever let her work her way into his heart? She'd caused him nothing but grief, nothing but trouble. He stiffened as Esteban took her by the arm and led her away.

He knew how the guard felt about her, but he also knew he wouldn't act on those feelings yet. Not until Baltasar's use for her was over. Peter waited for Baltasar to leave before moving out of his hiding place. Emily might have just given him the opportunity he'd been waiting for. While she and Baltasar were on their walk in the gardens, he would be in Baltasar's office, downloading his computer files and trying to find out any information he could on who this mysterious contact was in Colorado Springs.

He walked back to his bungalow, grabbed a bite and took a quick shower to wash off the jungle muck. As he stood under the hot spray, hazel eyes and long wheat-colored hair flashed through his mind. He had been in the jungle too long, he realized. He'd been so tempted to give in to her, to pull her into his arms and take her back. To believe that they really could make it work together. But he would have been fooling himself, and he might be a lot of things, but a fool wasn't one of them.

Exactly one hour later, he made his way back to the estate house and watched until he spotted Emily and Baltasar come out of the hospital wing with Marcos. Emily looked tired and flushed as she pushed the boy's wheelchair. The climate must be getting to her. He watched her for a moment, wondering how he was going to keep her safe in spite of herself, then headed for Baltasar's office. He needed to get as much information as he could, before the deal went down in Chicago. If anything went wrong, he wouldn't get another chance. He glanced at his watch. He had exactly three hours until Baltasar received his report back from Chicago.

He stood outside the French doors leading into Baltasar's empty office. He opened the door and slipped inside. As quickly as he could, he pulled out a disk drive and USB cable and plugged it in to Baltasar's computer. He scanned the files and, one by one, started downloading the folders onto the disk drive.

While the files were copying, he searched the desk, looking for anything that would help them nail *El Patrón.* In the third drawer, he hit pay dirt. For the last couple of years, Baltasar had been building an extensive network of mules to distribute his product worldwide. What Peter found especially interesting were the names: Anita, Rosa, Maria, Anna, Melinda. The mules were all women.

He took out a small camera used specifically by operatives for photographing documents and took several pictures of the pages in the file — the drop points and the photographs of the women. He had almost finished when he heard a door slam down the hallway.

He stiffened, and with his pulse racing he quickly restored order to the desk and returned the file. He disconnected the cable and disk drive and placed them with the camera in a small fanny pack as he slipped out the French doors. He had just hidden the pack in the bushes when Snake entered the room.

Crouching down, Peter watched Snake slowly peruse the office. His fingers lightly touched the desk, straightening the blotter before he crossed the room to the doors and peered out the glass. Peter dropped back farther into the bushes and held his breath as Snake stood motionless. After a minute, he reached down and turned the lock, then left the room.

Peter's breathing returned to normal. He waited a full minute before standing and walking casually out of the bushes. He would come back after nightfall and retrieve the fanny pack.

"Hey, you! What are you doing over there?"

Peter froze at the sound of the harsh voice. He took a deep breath then turned. One of Baltasar's guards had his weapon pointed at Peter's chest.

"Amigo," Peter said, raising his hands in the air. "No need to overreact." He smiled, though he recognized the guard as the man who was upset with Emily. Esteban — the little man with the huge ego.

"What you doing outside the boss's office?" he demanded in halting English.

"Waiting for Mr. Escalante," Peter said casually. He started to walk forward, to move as far away from the fanny pack as he could.

Esteban waved his gun, stopping him. "In the bushes?" His eyes narrowed suspiciously. "Let's go." He gestured Peter toward the path.

"Where?" Peter asked, and hardened his jaw to keep his cool as Esteban shoved the gun's muzzle into his back.

"You want to see the boss, now you gonna."

★ ★ ★

The heat was getting to Emily. Either that or she was getting sick, but she couldn't shake the lethargy that was overcoming her, nor the headache the blinding sun beating down on her head was producing. *Please don't let me get sick now,* but even as she said the silent prayer, her throat hurt as she swallowed.

She took a deep gulp off her water bottle and pulled her hat down over her head. She'd have to be extra careful around Marcos, whose limited immune system wouldn't be able to handle exposure to a virus right now.

She glanced down at the boy. His spirits were running high. He was chatting incessantly and wore a huge smile on his face. She attributed the change in his demeanor to the presence of his father more than anything else. The boy idolized Baltasar. It was sweet to see, but she wished the man was more deserving.

The two talked, completely unmoved by the overwhelming heat — nor did they seem to notice the constant presence of bugs circling around them. How could they casually stroll along as if there wasn't the danger of deadly snakes or hungry jaguars roaming on the other side of the mowed grass, just through the trees? She glanced at the thick foliage now, fully expecting something to jump out and attack them. Her head swam and she swayed on her feet.

"Dr. *Señorita?*"

Emily turned her attention back to Marcos. "I'm sorry, Marcos. What did you say?"

"You still don't look well, Dr. Armstrong," Baltasar said. "I hope you're not coming down with something."

"No, not at all," Emily denied, and stifled an urge to run her hand across her forehead. She didn't like the way he was looking at her and didn't think he would take very well to his son's doctor being sick, too. "It's the heat," she said. "I'm not used to this type of climate."

Before he could respond, they heard footsteps and turned to see Peter approaching with Esteban at his back. "Take Marcos back inside," Baltasar ordered softly.

Emily couldn't move. Something was wrong. Did that creep have a gun on Peter? Because Peter was letting him in.

"Now," Baltasar demanded.

She turned from Peter's stoic face and looked at Baltasar. The anger in his voice matched the cold fury in his eyes. "Yes, sir," she said, and quickly turned Marcos's chair away from the men.

"What is it?" Marcos said. "Why do we have to go in?"

"I don't know," Emily admitted, and didn't appreciate being put in the position to have to explain to the boy. Baltasar should have said something to his son, should have made up an excuse for cutting their walk short so Marcos wouldn't go back to his room worried and anxious.

"I guess he had unexpected business that couldn't wait." Emily glanced back over her shoulder, but all she could see were the three men standing close together talking. She couldn't see anything that would lead her to believe that Peter was in serious trouble. She supposed it was just the look on his face that had her stomach twisted into knots.

"Your papa's a very important man, and sometimes business can't be helped," she said, hoping to appease him.

Marcos nodded, but she could see the hurt in his eyes and it bothered her. Once she got him settled in his bed, she quickly and covertly took her temperature — 100.9. She cringed as she read the number, took some Tylenol and went in search of Robert. He would have to spend more time with the boy as she would need to keep her distance from Marcos, and she'd have to do so without Baltasar discovering why.

What if he found out? Worse yet, what if he decided he didn't need her anymore?

Peter played it cool and casual, explaining to Baltasar that he was just looking for him, making his way around the grounds, then hinted very subtly that perhaps his guard was a little too ambitious, a little too whacked. Baltasar wasn't buying it, though his gaze did sit on Esteban a little longer than was comfortable for the shifty guard.

"Let's go back to my office and wait for the news from Chicago," Baltasar said, and walked toward the house.

As Peter followed close behind, he prayed the CIA would come through for him and the drop in Chicago would go down as planned. He had hoped to get confirmation from his dad before he'd had to face Baltasar. A little advance warning in case the deal in Chicago went bad and he'd be able to grab Emily and disappear. But all bets were off now. It didn't appear as if Baltasar was going to let him out of his sight.

"Now that everything is settled, why don't I meet you back at your office?" Peter suggested. "I have a few phone calls I need to make, a little business I must take care of."

"I don't think so," Baltasar said casually.

"If I'm going to have Chicago ready for a major shipment on the thirteenth, I need to get people in place, payoffs have to be made."

"I understand that, Pietro, but I don't think you understand me. I want you to wait with me in my office for the news from Chicago."

"Why the hardball all of a sudden? We have time and I need to make sure everything is set up to go off without a hitch. If we're going to work together, then you're going to have to trust me, unless you don't want a piece of Chicago after all?"

Baltasar's gaze turned glacial. "You better hope everything goes off without a hitch, Mr. Presti." He opened the door and walked into his office, then sat behind his desk.

Peter followed him into the room and quickly scanned for any telltale signs that would betray his presence there earlier. Everything looked in order.

"Have a seat," Baltasar said, gesturing to the chair in front of his desk.

Not seeing any way around it, Peter sat down.

"I understand you paid a visit to Dr. Armstrong's room last night."

Peter's gut tightened. He stared at the man, trying to decide which way to spin what happened. "The woman's *muy bonita,* eh?" he said and gave Baltasar a wide toothy grin.

"She's my son's doctor," Baltasar said coldly.

"She's also an American," Peter explained. "And it's been a long time since I've talked to someone from home." The words came out more sincerely than he could have hoped, because to him Emily *was* home. *His* home. "I meant no disrespect."

"I understand there was a lot more than talking going on," Baltasar said, refusing to let it drop.

"She didn't seem to mind the attention. Why should you?" Peter questioned, hoping to put Baltasar on the defensive.

"I find it hard to believe Dr. Armstrong would let a total stranger kiss her."

She wouldn't. Peter shrugged. "I have that effect on women."

Baltasar scoffed and turned away. He took a cigar out of the humidor and, this time, didn't offer Peter one.

Things weren't boding well.

Baltasar rose, opened the door, murmured to Esteban then sat back down. Peter stared at the clock on his desk — ninety more minutes before he'd discover how the deal went down in Chicago, ninety more minutes before he'd find out if he'd live or die.

The silence in the room grew thick as the minutes ticked by. Peter took in every minute detail in the office, right down to the fibers on the carpet and the buzzing of a bee outside the window.

This wasn't going well.

A minute later, the door opened and Esteban walked into the room carrying a paper sack and looking at him with a small note of twisted triumph.

Anxiousness turned Peter's stomach.

"I asked Esteban to go through your bungalow and bring me back anything interesting."

Peter stiffened. "I hardly think that's an appropriate way to start off our working relationship."

"Neither is skulking about, spying, trespassing where you don't belong and seducing my son's doctor," Baltasar retorted. He dumped the bag out on the desk. Peter's wallet, phone, infrared goggles, knives and gun tumbled like a child's playthings across the wooden surface.

"This is an interesting collection," Baltasar said as he thumbed through the wallet, "but nothing unexpected."

The tension in Peter's back loosened a bit. There wasn't anything there that would incriminate him. Esteban hadn't found the global positioning system or the bugging devices he had stashed in the bungalow. His invasion could even have been a stroke of luck, he thought as he stared at his phone — if Baltasar let him answer it when the call came through. Of course, that didn't mean he'd be able to escape, if the news was bad. But at least he'd have forewarning on his side.

Baltasar handed Peter the wallet, then swept the knives, gun and goggles into one of his desk drawers.

"Mind telling me why you're keeping those?" Peter asked.

"Because where you're going, you won't be needing them."

Peter's hope that he'd be able to salvage this situation took a nosedive. "I thought we had a mutual exclusive business arrangement."

"We do," Baltasar said. "And as long as you play by the rules — *my* rules — we will get along just fine. But you need to under-stand that snooping around in my business is not acceptable."

"Fine. But keep in mind that you're not the only one taking risks here. I, too, have a lot at stake and don't plan on losing."

Baltasar stood, picked up Peter's phone, dropped it on the ground, and then stomped on it, pulverizing the plastic.

Peter stared at his lifeline in horrified shock.

"What did you do that for?"

"Because right now we're going to play things my way. Esteban is going to escort you to my private airstrip, Mr. Presti, where you will board my private plane that will take you to Caracas. In Caracas, you will book yourself on the next available plane to Chicago. If my little test goes down today as it should, then I will contact you and we will do business. If it doesn't, well I'm sure you're going to wish you never heard the name Baltasar Escalante. I hope I've made myself clear."

"Very clear. Everything will go down ex-actly the way it should. I have faith in my people."

"For both our sakes, I hope it does, too." He nodded to Esteban, and before Peter could make another sound, the little minion pulled him out of his chair and pushed him out the door. "If you're right and our little deal goes well, be ready for another shipment in twenty-four hours. I plan on taking Chicago by storm."

Twenty-four hours? Peter nodded and let several armed guards lead him to the airstrip, realizing that he would have to leave the fanny pack behind and hope no one would find it. He also accepted, with growing trepidation, that Emily was on her own. There was nothing he could do for her now.

Chapter Seven

Peter didn't make a sound as Esteban and another of Baltasar's guards escorted him off Baltasar's plane and into the main terminal at Caracas Bolivar International Airport. They had a five-hour wait for the next available flight to Chicago. Peter cringed. Five hours wasted sitting here with these goons, trying to formulate a plan that would get Emily out of Venezuela, yet not jeopardize his mission. This was one feat he didn't know how he'd be able to pull off, but he couldn't leave Emily to the mercy of a madman like Baltasar.

As he leaned back in his chair, he scanned the terminal, mentally targeting every exit and every potential threat. He spotted at least three of Baltasar's men scattered throughout the large room who were a little too interested in him. At one o'clock, Esteban's cell phone rang. Peter watched Esteban's face and prepared to bolt if the news was bad. To his surprise, Esteban handed him the phone. "*Sí,*" he said into the receiver.

"Mr. Presti. Congratulations." Baltasar's voice boomed in his ear.

Peter let out the breath he'd been holding and relaxed into the chair.

"The deal in Chicago went down exactly as it should have. Welcome to La Mano Oscura."

Peter shook his head. "I told you it wouldn't be a problem."

"As you'll soon discover, in our business it pays to be on guard. Get back to Chicago as soon as you can. The next shipment will be arriving tomorrow, same time, same place."

Peter nodded. "My flight leaves at six o'clock."

"Perfect. I'm going to enjoy working with you, Pietro. I like your spunk."

"Gracias," Peter said, and handed the phone back to Esteban.

Esteban nodded something then ended the call.

"The boss wants me to leave you here." He gave Peter a look that told him he didn't agree, but had no other choice.

Peter nodded as the two men got up and left. He watched them until they disappeared from his view, then leaned back in the hard plastic orange chair and considered what he would do next. He knew the CIA would want him to get to Chicago as ordered and capture Baltasar's mules when they arrived at the hotels with the drugs.

But he couldn't leave Emily here alone.

Nor could he go back to the estate.

He needed to contact his dad. He stared at the long row of pay phones on the wall. If his dad ordered him to rescue Emily, it would justify the counter-mission he was plotting. He strolled toward the phones, looking around for Baltasar's informants. If they were still there, he couldn't see them.

He took a deep breath and turned away from the phones. This was a chance he couldn't take. If someone traced the call, he'd lead them right to his parents' house. He took his duffel bag filled with the clothes Esteban had packed for him and disappeared into the men's room.

He changed and shaved, and after the bathroom emptied, he quickly shaved his head, watching as the long brown hair dropped onto the counter. By the time he was finished, there wasn't more than an inch of hair on his head. He quickly flushed the hair and dumped the duffel bag, then walked out of the bathroom in his new cover, his new persona — Peter Vance.

Casually, he walked through the airport and hailed a cab. "The San Marquis hotel, please," he said in perfect English.

"No luggage, *señor?*" the cab driver asked.

"The airline lost it," he responded, and watched out the window as they wound their way through the tall buildings of Caracas and to the San Marquis Hotel. At a pay phone in the lobby, Peter punched in the number for the hotel's reservation line and booked a room for Peter Vance using a credit card number he'd memorized. As he checked in, he promised the clerk a credit card imprint once the airline delivered his luggage. It worked like a charm.

Once in his room, he sat on the bed, picked up the phone and made a collect call to his father.

"What happened? I couldn't reach you," Max said.

"I lost my phone."

His father hesitated a moment. "The Chicago drop went off as planned."

"I heard. Thanks."

"Where are you?"

"At the San Marquis Hotel in Caracas." Peter quickly explained everything that had happened that morning.

"All right, get to Chicago as planned.

After you make the pickup from the mules, we'll move in and arrest them."

"You'll need to implement it without me."

"Peter, it's your job, your mission. You have to be there."

"Pietro Presti has disappeared."

"What are you talking about?"

"I had to lose the cover to get out of the airport and make contact."

"Fine, you get to Chicago, get a wig and get back in character before any of Baltasar's men see you or you'll never be able to work that territory again."

"I need you to order me to go back for Emily."

Max hesitated. "Peter, I can't do that. Let me handle it. The raid has been moved up. That compound is going to be swarming with agents at midnight tonight. We'll be able to get her out."

Peter looked at the clock on the nightstand. "That's eight hours from now. Anything could happen in eight hours, especially where Emily is concerned."

"I realize you've been working on your own for a while now, but we're a team. You need to trust us to take care of our own. We'll get her out."

Peter hesitated, trying to find the best

way to explain. "Emily seems to have a knack for getting into trouble. I can't leave her alone."

Max blew out a frustrated breath. "Don't blow your cover, Peter. Don't blow your career."

"Sorry, Dad, but right now I can't see any other way. Baltasar's on to her, and he's coming apart at the seams, acting irrationally, angry and suspicious one minute, charming and reasonable the next."

"If you defy my orders, you'd better help ensure this raid goes off as planned and we get Baltasar, or there won't be anything we can do to help you and Emily. You realize that?"

"It's a chance I have to take."

"Even if it means the end of your career?"

Peter closed his eyes and took a deep breath. He loved the CIA, he loved the satisfaction he gained when a mission came together and he knew he'd made a difference in the world. Yeah, he loved his job, but he'd never stopped loving Emily and he wouldn't take a chance with her life.

"Sometimes a Vance has to do what a Vance has to do, and sometimes he has to go it alone."

After several hours of rest, Emily woke feeling a little better, though her throat was still scratchy. She drank down another glass of water and took two more Tylenols. It was well past the dinner hour and very dark out. She worried that Baltasar might have been looking for her.

She took a quick shower, dressed, then searched for Robert. She found him in the kitchen, finishing up a late dinner. "Hi," she said quietly as she walked into the room.

"Your dinner is in the fridge."

"Thanks, I'm not that hungry. Has Baltasar been here? Was he looking for me?"

"No, you're okay. He's been absent most of the day. I think something major is going down."

"Really, why?"

"It's been real quiet around here and most of the guards are gone, but there's been a lot of noise coming from the far end of the estate behind the house."

Emily couldn't help wondering what was up, and whether or not it would involve them. She wished she could talk to Peter, but she hadn't seen him since she'd left him and Baltasar on the lawn earlier. Worry blossomed inside her. She had to trust that he was okay.

"How are you feeling?" Robert asked.

"A little better."

"You look better. Keep taking the Tylenol, you need to be on your toes."

"I know."

"Robert," she started then looked around her. She wondered if Esteban was lurking somewhere, or if someone was listening or watching them. She lowered her voice. "If I had discovered a way off the compound, would you come with me?"

Robert stilled. "What do you mean?"

"Through the jungle back to Caracas."

"In a heartbeat."

"Really?" she said, surprised. "Even though it would mean going into the jungle?"

Robert nodded. "We have to face the fact that Baltasar isn't going to let us leave here alive." The certain knowledge weighed heavy in his gaze.

"How can you be so sure?" she asked, not wanting to accept his words.

"If Baltasar let us go, his actions would become an international incident, not just for Doctors Without Borders, but also for the federal government. You can't just kidnap American citizens, hold them against their will, and hope nobody bats an eye. It would be a lot easier — and a lot less messy — for him to just arrange an *accident*."

The full implication of his logic hit home. She'd had those same thoughts herself, but she hadn't wanted to believe it, hadn't accepted their fate as calmly as Robert seemed to have. She supposed it was because deep down she knew that as long as Peter was there, he wouldn't let anything happen to her.

She'd been such a fool.

"Tell me you weren't just speaking hypothetically," Robert asked as a bright sheen of hope filled his eyes.

She scooted closer to him, placing her arm up on his shoulder and whispering in his ear in a way that would have any onlookers think that perhaps the two doctors were more than friends, but at least they wouldn't be able to hear what she said. As quickly as she could, she told him about the motorcycle on the other side of the wall. "We should leave at dawn so we can see our way down that mountain."

"We should leave now," Robert countered.

"We can't take the chance of getting stuck out there at night. What if we went the wrong way? Instead of finding the ocean, we'd find ourselves hopelessly lost deep in the jungle."

"You're right," he relented. "Get a good night's sleep, and I'll meet you here at sunrise."

She stood. "All right. I'll check on Marcos."

"Okay. And Em?"

She turned back.

"How'd you find out?"

She smiled. "It's a long story. I'll tell it to you in the morning."

He stood, then headed down the hall whistling a jolly tune.

When Emily entered Marcos's room, she was surprised to find him looking so pale. It seemed to be taking all his energy just to breathe. "Marcos!" She hurried to his bedside. She checked his chart and saw that the nurse had given him a fast-acting pain medication for break-through pain, on top of the controlled release morphine in his intravenous line. The poor child had taken a severe turn for the worse since their outing that afternoon.

Marcos opened his eyes as she sat by his side. "Dr. *Señorita?*"

"*Sí,* Marcos, I'm here."

"I dreamed about my mama."

"You did? Was it a happy dream?"

He nodded. "She's waiting for me."

Unbidden tears filled Emily's throat. She

swallowed, forced them back down then took a deep breath to steady her emotions. "Are you feeling okay? Does it hurt?"

He nodded, but he already had so much of the drug in his small body that she was afraid to give him anymore.

"Would you like me to sing to you?" she asked, hoping for that spark of enthusiasm. Unfortunately, it wasn't forthcoming. He looked so tired.

"Will you pray with me?" he asked.

She nodded and took his little hand. She watched him close his eyes, and tried to speak over the lump in her throat. She closed her eyes, too, and when she spoke it was with her whole heart. "Dear Lord, please look after our Marcos. Make him strong, take away his pain so he can rest, but most of all, Lord, walk with him so he isn't afraid."

"And tell my mama I love her," he whispered.

"Amen," Emily said softly, and kept her eyes shut for a long moment so he wouldn't see the sheen of her tears. She was his doctor; she had to be strong for him. But here on this estate, she couldn't leave, she couldn't go home and distance herself from the horror of death, she couldn't spend the night in her own bed and regroup her emotions so she was able to separate herself from the pain and heartache of watching such a sweet child die.

She laid her head on the side of his bed and watched the rise and fall of his chest as he struggled to fill his lungs with air.

"Dr. Armstrong?" Baltasar called softly from the doorway. She turned to him and was surprised to see the fear on his face and the dejected slump of his shoulders. There was nothing strong or intimidating about this man now. He just looked like a father afraid for his son.

She reached out her hand to him. He stepped forward and took it. "Marcos isn't feeling very well. Would you like to sit here with him? He needs you right now."

Baltasar nodded. She stood and he took her place on the stool next to his child's bed.

"Marcos?" Baltasar said softly.

Marcos's eyes fluttered open. "Papa?"

Baltasar smiled. The look on his face broke her heart. However bad this man was, he did love his son. There must be goodness inside him somewhere.

"Papa, would you tell me the story about when I was born?" Marcos asked.

Baltasar nodded, and scooted closer.

"Your mama was such a beautiful and brave woman. There wasn't another like her in all of Venezuela. Her name was Bianca, but I called her *flor de la selva,* because her beauty rivaled that of the most vibrant flowers in the heart of the jungle."

Marcos smiled, his lips quivering as he finished the line with his papa. Obviously this was an often told and much loved story. For this one moment, Marcos looked happy. He looked as if the pain wasn't too much to bear.

Someone cleared his throat from the doorway. Emily turned and was surprised to see Esteban. Not now, she thought. *Please, Lord, Marcos needs his daddy.*

"What is it?" Baltasar said, and she could tell by the irritation in his tone that he wasn't any happier to see Esteban than she was.

"They need you at the airstrip, sir."

Emily saw the crestfallen look settle over Marcos's face and felt disappointment weigh heavily on her shoulders.

Baltasar turned to his son, thought for a moment, then turned back to Esteban. "I can't go now. I'm with my son. Tell Snake to cover for me and I'll get there when I can."

Emily let out the deep breath she hadn't

been aware of holding. *Thank you, Lord.*

"*Sí, señor,*" Esteban said, but before he turned to leave, he looked her over, his gaze sweeping down her body, his eyes filling with cold, dark contempt.

Emily ignored him. "Can I get you a cup of coffee?" she asked Baltasar once Esteban left to do his bidding.

"That would be wonderful. Thank you," Baltasar said sincerely and, at that moment, he wasn't a drug lord or a kidnapper, he was the father of one of her patients — a patient who was about to die.

Filled with a heavy heart, Emily walked into the kitchen and started a fresh pot of coffee. When she felt someone's presence lurking behind her, she whirled then gasped. "Peter!" She stared at him as familiarity gave regret a fresh squeeze. He looked so much like *her* Peter. "Your hair. Your face." She took a step forward and had to stop herself from touching his clean-shaven skin.

"Come on, Emily, we need to go," Peter said softly.

"I can't."

His face darkened. "Don't say that, Emily. I've risked everything to come back and get you. Don't cause me any trouble now."

His words tore at her. She touched his arm. "Peter, I don't mean to cause you trouble. Really. Baltasar is in the other room with his son." She looked down at the floor. "Marcos has taken a severe turn. I don't think he'll last the night. I need to stay here with him." She looked into Peter's eyes, imploring him to understand.

"You must come with me." He held out his hand. He'd been through too much to turn around and leave her here now. If the boy was going to die, there wasn't anything more she could do for him. It was a harsh thought, but a practical one. The child's life couldn't be saved, but theirs still could. He wasn't about to leave there without her.

"Baltasar's expecting me back in a few minutes," Emily whispered, and glanced toward the door. "Let me go back to him and bring him his coffee, then I'll slip away as soon as I can. I promise."

"A plane is coming in to pick us up. It won't wait. When it leaves, we have to be on it. It's our last chance. Our only chance. Is that clear?"

She nodded. "Perfectly. I don't want to fight you, but if I don't go back in there, Baltasar will get suspicious. He'll come looking for me. There isn't an excuse I can give for disappearing right now. Not at this point in Marcos's illness."

Peter nodded. He understood, but he wasn't happy about it.

"I'm sorry I've made things so difficult, Peter. You were right. Robert and I should have taken our chances with the motorcycle."

He raised his eyebrows in surprise and wondered where the change in heart had come from. She loved to make his life difficult, she always had.

"I won't stay long. I just need a little more time, to appease Baltasar."

"All right, I'll take Dr. Fletcher to the airstrip with me now, but I'm coming back for you in exactly thirty minutes. Meet me out back and don't be late."

"I won't."

"I mean it, Emily. This is our last chance." He hurried to Dr. Robert Fletcher's room, opened his door and slipped inside. After a moment of explaining who he was and what he was doing there, Robert eagerly followed Peter out of the hospital wing. If only Emily could have been that cooperative, Peter thought. His life would be so much easier. But he supposed she had a point, no use riling up Baltasar before the plane arrived.

They crept around the compound, stopping every now and then to listen for guards, but they didn't need to be so covert. The place was empty. "Everyone must be at the airstrip awaiting the shipment," Peter said. He quickly skirted the side of the compound until he came to the bushes outside Baltasar's office.

He bent down and stuck his hand in the bush where he'd hidden his pack. It was still there. He heaved a huge sigh then turned to Robert. "Stay here, I'll be back in a second." He picked the lock on Baltasar's office doors, then ran to the desk and pulled open the drawer where Baltasar had stashed his infrared goggles, gun and knives. He slipped the goggles around his neck, then shoved the other items into his pockets and slipped back out the door.

"Let's go," he said.

"Where?" Robert asked as he followed him off the path and into the jungle.

"Home."

Chapter Eight

Peter and Robert hid in the bushes and watched the activity on the airstrip. A large truck with a canvas-covered back was parked off to the side. Several of Baltasar's guards unloaded and opened crates stored in the back of the truck. They pulled plastic baggies filled with white powder out of the crates and loaded them into large black duffel bags.

"This is quite an impressive operation," Robert said.

"Each duffel will hold about fifty kilos. He's planning on dumping five hundred kilos into Colorado Springs."

"That's incredible," Robert muttered.

"And the root cause of all the problems the Springs has been facing lately, especially in the last few months."

Suddenly, lights along the runway lit up, and far in the distance Peter could see the twinkling glow of an approaching plane.

"What are we doing here?" Robert asked. "Do you have a car stashed close by? And where's Emily?"

"She's still with Marcos. Don't worry, by tomorrow morning we'll all be back in Colorado and you'll be eating breakfast with your wife and kids."

"From your lips to God's ears," Robert said softly.

"Stay out of sight," Peter commanded as the plane approached the runway. He moved in as close to the airstrip as he could without being seen. The plane landed with a loud screech and rolled to a stop not fifty feet in front of him. Several of Baltasar's guards started running toward the plane.

The fuselage doors flew open and agents poured out onto the runway, diving into the jungle, moving out of the line of fire. Understanding what was happening, Baltasar's guards started calling out warnings, guns were raised and shots fired. From his position in the bushes, Peter started firing, giving as much cover to the agents fleeing the plane as he could.

A unit in black swung around behind him, popping up from the thick foliage to fire on the guards. Once all the agents were on the ground, Peter hurried back for Robert. "Follow me," he called, and they both ran toward the plane.

As they approached, Peter noticed most

of Baltasar's guards had fallen, but there was still sporadic gunfire in the jungle. What concerned him was that he hadn't yet seen Baltasar. The man must still be back at the compound with Emily. That was one complication Peter hadn't planned on. He didn't like the idea of Emily alone with Baltasar once the guns started firing. Who knew how he'd react?

He helped Robert into the plane, then climbed up behind him and quickly took off his pack. Jake Montgomery, FBI computer expert and one of his best friends, dropped his helmet onto his seat as he saw them. "Finally! I've been waiting for you."

A large smile spread across Peter's face as he stared at his friend. "Good to see you, too."

Jake cocked a grin. "I knew you were out there causing trouble somewhere."

"Yep, and I'm still not done." He handed Jake the pack. "There's a disk drive in there with the computer files I was able to download off Baltasar's computer. We believe there's another agent of Baltasar's working in the Springs, but I haven't been able to determine who he is yet. I really hope the information is on that disk."

Jake nodded. "I'll get right on it."

"This is Dr. Fletcher. He needs a lift back to the States."

Robert sat down and immediately strapped himself in. Peter turned toward the door.

"Wait a minute," Jake said. "Where are you going? I have orders to bring you back. Your dad has a plane standing by to take you directly to Chicago. He said it's important that you be there in the morning. The rest of the team will stay here and round up what's left of Baltasar's agents."

Peter looked into Jake's face and realized that his dad had given him one last chance to save his career. "Emily's still back at the house, Jake. I won't leave her."

"You can trust me. I'll get her."

"Jake, I love you like a brother, but I can't. We'll be back. Both of us." With that, Peter jumped out of the plane's opening and disappeared into the jungle. He promised Emily he'd come back for her, and he wouldn't let her down.

Emily's heart kicked up a notch as she heard the sounds of an approaching plane. She had to think up an excuse to get out of there. She couldn't miss that plane. Peter must be outside waiting for her now. She glanced over at Baltasar. He was reading aloud from a storybook, not seeming to notice the noise from the aircraft, or that Marcos no longer had his eyes open. As if his voice alone could keep Marcos there with him. She supposed on some level the sound of his father's reading must be a comfort, though she couldn't help wondering if Marcos could even hear him any longer.

Suddenly Marcos's eyes flew open.

The boy reached for his father, then his eyes widened and he went still, his hand dropping away. The monitor started an even, relentless tone, ringing through the room.

Then the gunfire began.

Baltasar stood, the book falling to the floor with a resounding thud.

Emily rushed forward.

Baltasar turned to her. "Do something!"

"I can't. There's nothing."

"Don't say that! Do something now!"

Shocked, she stared at his bulging eyes, his flushed skin, his breath coming in quick harsh gasps. "There's nothing," she said in her most professional voice. "He's gone. He's not suffering any longer. There's no more fear, no more pain."

"Don't say that! Bring him back," he ordered.

"I can't."

He pulled a gun out of his pocket and pushed it against her temple. "You will or you'll die."

Desperate, Emily turned to Marcos and began to pump on his chest. Tears streamed down her face at the feel of his little body beneath her hands. She knew it was too late, knew there was nothing she could do to save him. She also knew it was better for Marcos where he was, with the Lord and his mother and away from the pain and sickness.

She felt Baltasar's menacing presence behind her, heard his breathing grow raspier with each breath. She pumped over and over on Marcos's chest, and still the monitor blared on. "There's nothing I can do," she pleaded.

Baltasar flew into a rage, knocking over carts, tearing pictures off the walls, screaming. The harsh sounds of tortured grief echoed through the room. She flinched, jumping at each outburst. Her tears caught on the fear rising in her throat. She choked on them then coughed as she continued to pump on Marcos's unmoving chest.

"You're sick!" Baltasar bellowed. "You did this. You shouldn't have gone near him. You knew his immune system was weak. You killed him."

"No!" she stepped away from the child. "I didn't. I cared for him. Don't do this!"

He moved toward her, cold fury in his eyes. Emily felt the wall at her back as she moved to escape him. But there was no escape, she was cornered.

Esteban came running through the doorway. "We have to go, *señor!* There are U.S. agents all over the compound. They've confiscated the merchandise!"

Emily looked from Baltasar to Esteban. The plane. It was full of agents. She was saved. She blew out a deep breath.

Confusion filled Baltasar's horrified expression. "N-no," he stammered. "You're mistaken. It cannot be."

"I'm sorry, *señor.* There is no mistake. I've seen them myself. We must leave, immediately. I have a Jeep out front with your computer and important files loaded in the back."

Baltasar didn't move. He stared, unblinking.

"Señor?"

Then something diabolical snapped behind his eyes, and he became alert, his gaze cruel and deadly.

"Gracias, Esteban," he said, his tone once again even, his stature straight and in

control. He hurried past the guard and out of the room.

Emily's shoulders sagged with relief as she watched him go.

"Bring the doctor," he called over his shoulder as he disappeared around the corner.

Emily's gaze shot to Esteban. A large leering grin split his face. Her mind filled with numbing coldness. He walked toward her. Panic threatened to consume her. She looked around, searching for anything she could use to stop him. She stared at the mess strewn all over the floor from Baltasar's rampage. But they were just objects, she couldn't seem to get her mind to think, to focus on any one thing. He stepped close, reaching.

"Oh, Lord, please," she cried and backed away from him.

"The Lord can't save you now, *chiquita*."

She couldn't let that man touch her. Wouldn't. She'd rather die right there in that room than out in the jungle at the mercy of Baltasar and his twisted sidekick.

Esteban lunged. Emily threw the intravenous cart against him. She ran past him, but he grabbed hold of her shirt. The fabric ripped, but still held. He had her. She looked at Marcos and thought how hard he'd fought for his life, thought about how much love he had in his heart, and how that love had kept him going. She wouldn't give up.

She whipped around and kicked Esteban in the stomach as hard as she could. As he doubled over, she picked up a lead crystal vase and crashed it onto his head. Then she ran, pulling as many items behind her into his path as she could find as she sped down the hallway and toward the back door.

She knew how Esteban felt about her, remembered well the smell of his rancid breath on her neck. At this point, she would rather face the biggest snake, cat or spider in the jungle than be left to the mercy of that beast.

"Please Lord, please let me make it into the jungle," she prayed as she ran out the door.

"I'm going to get you, *chiquita*," Esteban yelled and she knew he would give everything he had to get his hands on her.

Peter was right; there are worse things out there than the creatures in the jungle. She told herself that over and over again as she left the manicured lawns, bursting through the bushes and moving far away from the cobblestone path.

Where was Peter? He said he'd meet her out back, but he wasn't there!

"Chiquita?" Esteban called in a high-pitched mocking tone. A tone that told her it didn't matter where she went, or how far she'd run, he would find her.

He did have an advantage. He knew every square inch of the estate. He probably even knew which trees the snakes and jaguars lived in.

A branch swiped painfully at her cheek as she made her way toward the sounds of gunfire and the lights of the runway. Peter must still be there. He must not have been able to get away; otherwise he would have been there to help her. He wouldn't have left her to the mercy of Baltasar. She believed that with all her heart. Why hadn't she taken her chances with him? Why did she ever go back into that room? Why couldn't she listen to someone who tried to give her advice? To guide her?

Because she had to be in control, she thought bitterly. She ran, her legs pumping, her mind racing, her body trembling. Maybe that's why she'd never fully given her heart to the Lord like so many of her friends had done. To relinquish herself that much . . . it was something she'd never been able to do. Being in control of her own actions, her own destiny, was everything to her. And look how much that control was costing her now.

"I see you, *chiquita*." Esteban's voice skittered down her spine like the many legs of a spider scurrying after a kill.

She heard the engines of a plane revving and pushed herself to move faster, holding her arms out in front of her to knock away anything in her path and hoped she'd be moving too fast for anything icky to stick.

She saw lights up ahead, and prayed she was almost there. She burst through the last bush and pushed into a clearing, and stared in horror as the plane raced down the runway and rose into the sky.

Peter?

Oh God, he wouldn't have left without her, would he?

"*Chiquita,* I see you!"

Where would she go? What would she do now? The motorcycle, it was her only hope. She would climb the wall, and even in the dark, she would ride the motorcycle through the jungle and get as far away from Esteban and Baltasar as she could.

Before she could duck back into the bushes, a hand clasped over her mouth. Her eyes bulged in terror as she was slammed against a hard chest and pulled into the brush. In horror, she realized this hand was different — rougher, thinner, drier, and the chest was not warm or protective. This was not her Peter.

She fought the fear threatening to overwhelm her and felt her knees weaken as her mind went numb. *Oh, please, Lord, not Esteban.*

Peter ran back to the spot he'd told Emily to meet him. He knew the plane wouldn't wait much longer and if they didn't want to be stranded in South America, then they needed to be on that plane. "Emily," he called softly.

No answer.

He circled around to the front of the hospital wing, hoping to glance through a window, to see if she was still in Marcos's room. As he approached, he saw a Jeep parked out front, but no sign of a guard, Baltasar or Emily. He entered the wing and ran to Marcos's room, then stood in the doorway, shocked by the equipment and medical supplies smashed and broken on the floor.

The child was lying in the bed, his eyes wide open and staring at nothing. Peter approached him and pulled the sheet up over his head, then said a silent prayer. Suddenly, he heard Baltasar bellowing for Snake and Esteban. "Bring me those doctors who killed my son!"

Peter cringed at the crashing sounds throughout the house. Baltasar was completely out of control, but at least he didn't have Emily yet, which meant they still had hope. He hurried forward then stopped as Baltasar loomed in the doorway, his face riddled with confusion. "Pietro?"

"That's right, Baltasar."

"What are you doing here?"

"I'm here to bring you to justice."

Baltasar stared at him for a long moment then let loose a loud laugh. "No, Mr. Presti, or whatever your name is. You're here to die." He pulled a gun out of his pocket but before he could take aim, Peter dove, flying into Baltasar, knocking him off balance. The gun went off, the bullet piercing the wall. They both fell to the floor in the hallway, rolling, fists flailing, legs kicking. Peter got in a good punch that left Baltasar dazed and reeling. He shoved the muzzle of his gun under Baltasar's chin.

"You get up real slow and I'll let you live, although for what you did to Emily and Robert, I'd prefer to blow your head off right here."

Baltasar's hate-filled eyes focused on his. "You'd do well to blow my head off, Mr. Presti. It's the only thing that's going to save you."

"Big talk for a man on his back."

"It won't be long before you're on your back, begging me for mercy. You and that little doctor friend of yours."

Peter smiled. "Get up." He stood back as Baltasar rose then led him into the kitchen where he tied him to a chair. "I've wanted to muzzle you for days now," Peter said as he placed a large piece of tape over Baltasar's mouth. "My friends will be here soon, to escort you to a nice jail where your only companions will be rats and roaches."

Baltasar scoffed through the tape.

Peter didn't like the look in his eyes. The man should be concerned, he should be worried that his entire organization was crumbling around him; instead he had a look of triumph, as if he knew something Peter didn't.

Prudence and experience dictated he should stay with him until the other agents arrived. It would be a mistake to let this animal out of his sight, but he had to find Emily. He had to find her before Snake or Esteban did.

Without looking back, he tore out the front of the house and once again circled around back. He heard the plane making its way down the runway. It was leaving without them.

He ran toward the airstrip. Had she gone without him? There was no sign of her anywhere. And worse, every one of the agents he'd passed hadn't seen her, either.

The motorcycle.

Perhaps she'd recognized how desperate her situation was, put aside her earlier reservations and done what she should have done before — climbed that wall and rode to safety. He ran through the jungle heading toward the wall, hoping and praying.

As he reached the wall, he quickly climbed to the top and looked down. The motorcycle was still where he'd left it.

Frustration teetering on panic filled him. Where could she be? He took out his infrared night-vision goggles and scanned back inside the compound, but saw only agents tracking down the remaining guards and storming the estate. Hopefully they'd find Baltasar and he could put that worry behind him once and for all. But where was Emily?

As he continued to scan the area, his

breath caught as he focused the goggles on a man pushing the small frame of a woman into a Jeep, before climbing behind the wheel and driving away from the estate.

Emily!

Chapter Nine

Panic clutched hold of Peter's heart. He jumped down from the wall, pulled the motorcycle out from behind the bush and tore off after the Jeep. Peter's hands clutched the handlebars as he flew down the dark road, his night-vision infrared goggles showing him the way. He took several deep breaths, squeezing and releasing the handlebar grips, trying to rein in the overwhelming urge to ride up on the Jeep and take out the driver. He had to play it safe and make sure whoever was driving that Jeep didn't hurt Emily.

Biding his time and wrestling a strong hold on his patience, Peter followed the Jeep hour after hour as it wound through the countryside down one dirt road after another. As dawn finally broke, he pulled off his infrared goggles as they entered a small village on the Orinoco River. Peter stopped his bike on the outskirts of the village and hid it behind a bush. He stood back and watched to see who would get out of the Jeep. Snake! Peter took a deep breath and watched as he and Emily walked into a small thatched hut.

From what he could tell, she looked all right. Snake didn't have to pull her kicking and screaming into the small house. She was holding up a brave front. Pride swelled within him. That was his Em. He stuck to the bushes as long as he could, then pulled his gun and ran across the opening before throwing himself against the hut. He crashed through the front door, rolled, then leaped up onto one knee and aimed his gun squarely at Snake who was standing against the wall, arms raised, shock playing across his face.

"Emily, come stand behind me," Peter ordered. When she hadn't moved, Peter turned to her. She was staring at him in stupefied shock. "Come on, Em," he repeated.

"Good grief, Peter. What on earth is going on?" she sputtered.

"What does it look like is going on? I'm rescuing you."

Emily gripped her hips and rolled her eyes. "Peter, I'm perfectly fine. I don't need rescuing."

Peter stood and turned from Emily to Snake, who was just standing there, holding up his hands and nodding at him with his eyebrows cocked in a you're-such-a-bozo expression. Peter gritted his teeth to keep from roaring. "Would somebody mind telling me what's going on?"

Emily stepped forward. "Snake's sister needs a doctor, which is why he brought me here. That's who I was going to see before you decided to knock the door down and almost give me a heart attack."

Peter could see the irritation in her eyes; they always deepened to a dark umber-green when she was mad. Just the fact that he still remembered that made him want to throttle her. The woman still had no concept of where she was and the danger she was in. "Emily, step outside the door. We're leaving. Now."

"Peter, she needs me. I can't just abandon her."

Not again. Peter took a deep breath to steady his temper and stop himself from swinging her over his shoulder and carrying her off on his motorcycle like the Neanderthal she'd always accused him of being. In fact, he thought he was being quite patient and reasonable, considering he was exhausted, starving, and had been out of his mind with worry half the night. Why did he even bother trying?

"This is it, Emily. Either you get your

butt out that door and leave with me now or I'm going . . . I'm going to make you sorry you didn't." He finished flustered when he couldn't think of anything to threaten her with. He should leave her. It would serve her right if she had to get out of this mess on her own after all the trouble she'd caused him. Why hadn't he gone to Chicago like he was ordered? Instead he missed his ride and quite possibly lost his job.

Emily stiffened. "Fine. Go without me. I'm sure Snake will see that I get to safety." She turned to Snake, who gave her an imperceptible nod. "Where's your sister?"

He cocked his head toward the back door.

Peter cringed at the exchange. "He's Baltasar's main thug. He will turn you over to his boss the moment you're done here."

"Wasn't Baltasar captured back at the house?" Snake interrupted.

Peter looked at him for a minute before admitting that he wasn't sure. He turned back to Emily and glared. "I was too busy chasing after you to make sure he was arrested and detained properly. I see now what a colossal mistake that was."

Emily bit her lip.

At least she had the decency to look

sorry for giving him so much grief.

"Don't be so hard on her," Snake said. "I didn't give her much choice. My sister needs her."

Emily placed a hand on her forehead, tilted her head forward and closed her eyes. Suddenly Peter could see how tired she was. How pale. After a moment, she opened her eyes and said, "Listen, Peter. I realize you wanted me to wait for you in back of the hospital wing, but Esteban was chasing me and when I got there, you weren't there. I kept running toward the airstrip, but the plane had left without me. Esteban would have caught me, except Snake got to me first. After he explained how much his sister needed me, I decided to come here and see if I could help. Surely you can understand how I'd have to help? How I didn't see any other choice?"

Her watery gaze implored him to understand. And he did, but that didn't mean he had to like it.

"We couldn't chance going back for you," Snake added. "All of Baltasar's guards were on the lookout for the doctors."

"He blames us for Marcos's death," Emily said.

"I know," Peter said dryly. He turned to

174

Snake. "Just where do you fit into this whole game?"

"I don't. My sister needs help, I saw an opportunity and I took it. Now if you don't mind, I'd like to check on my sister."

Peter didn't buy the concerned brother act. "How do you plan on repaying Emily for her help?"

"By making sure she gets out of the country without Baltasar's men finding her."

"I can do that," Peter said.

"If you plan on sticking around."

The two stared at each other, and Peter didn't like the challenge he saw in the other man's eyes. Just who was this guy? And what was his deal with Emily?

"To do that we need to find out for sure if Baltasar's in custody," Snake continued. "We can't let him find us."

"I don't have a way of contacting my people," Peter said, and wished Baltasar had just stashed his phone in the drawer with the rest of his stuff rather than smashing it into a million pieces.

Snake picked up his pack off the ground.

"Hold it," Peter said, raising his gun.

"Chill. It's all right. I'm just taking out my phone."

Peter nodded. "Slow and easy."

Snake pulled a satellite phone out of his pack and threw it.

Peter caught it in midair. "You're just full of surprises."

"I like life better that way."

Peter stared at him, trying to get a handle on the slippery man. "I just bet you do." He dialed his dad then leaned back against the wall. He'd been driving all night, was hungry and exhausted. "Hey," he said when Maxwell Vance answered the line.

"Peter, where are you?"

"I'd rather not say. I'm not sure how secure this line is."

"You have another problem."

Peter held his breath. "You mean other than the fact that I'm not where I'm supposed to be?"

"Baltasar escaped."

Guilt pricked him. He should have stayed. He should have made sure the other agents had Baltasar before leaving. Frustration tensed his shoulders and made him want to break something. Why wasn't anything going right? He gave the news to Emily and Snake through gritted teeth.

"And from all reports he's on a frenzied manhunt for you and Emily," Max added.

"Then we better make sure we're not still here when he arrives."

"That would be a wise move. He's got a lot of influence in the jungle. Emily's with you then?"

"Yes," Peter said and turned to look at her. She was just standing there, watching him with fear widening her eyes. Finally, her situation was beginning to dawn on her.

"Can you hide her somewhere safe?"

Peter's mind went blank. There was no place safe in the jungle.

"Get yourself to Baltasar's lab and see if you can find anything there. He removed the computer and all his files from the compound. Jake is working on the disk you gave him, but we need more. We need every shred of evidence you can find on this guy. We can't afford to let him slip through the cracks."

This was his fault, Peter thought. He had it all in the palm of his hand: Baltasar, the computer, the files, and he let it all go. He gave Baltasar the time he needed to destroy the evidence. "His lab won't be easy to find, even with the coordinates you gave me. I no longer have my GPS receiver. It's still in the bungalow back at the compound." He turned to Snake, his eyebrows raised in question to see if the man had any other surprises for him.

Snake shook his head. "But I can take you there," he offered.

Peter held back his surprise. "You'd take me to the lab?"

"Yep."

"In exchange for what?" Peter didn't bother to hide the suspicion in his voice.

"U.S. citizenship papers for my sister and her baby."

Peter thought for a moment. "How do I know I can trust you?"

"You don't."

"That's for sure." Peter explained Snake's offer to his dad, and what he wanted in return. He then handed Snake the phone so he could give Max the necessary information to obtain the papers.

After a minute, Snake disconnected the line. "He said he'd make it happen."

"Then he will."

"Then I guess we're working this thing together."

Peter cringed. Nothing like working with the enemy to brighten your day. "Guess so."

Emily picked up the medical bag Snake had grabbed for her back at the estate and walked into the back room, leaving the two men alone to discuss their business. She stopped inside the door to let her eyes adjust to the darkness and was at once overwhelmed by the musty smell. She hurried to the window, pulled back the small, dark blanket blocking out the light and stared at the thick sheet of plastic covering the opening. That would never do. She pulled down the plastic, letting the fresh air in. Only then did she turn to her patient lying on the bed.

Emily tried to hide her shock as she stared at the poor woman. She was so thin. Her cheeks had sunk leaving deep hollows in her face. Purple smudges outlined her dark brown eyes. The woman looked up at her with hope and fear shining through her face. "Did I hear my brother?" she asked with a shaky voice.

Emily forced herself to smile. "You did. He brought me here to take care of you. I'm Dr. Armstrong."

"An American?" she asked with confusion.

Emily nodded. "It's a long story and not one you need to worry about." There was a stack of small towels and a bucket of water sitting on a table in the corner. She approached the table, dipped a cloth into the water, then sat in a chair next to the bed and gently washed the woman's face. "Your brother said your name is Rosalia. That's a lovely name."

The woman closed her eyes and gave a slight smile. "*Gracias*. Is my baby going to be all right, doctor?"

"That's what we're going to find out. Is it all right if I examine you?"

Rosalia nodded, then squeezed her eyes shut as her breathing came in quick painful gasps.

Startled, Emily stood. "Are you in labor?"

"I think so. I've been having a lot of pain all night."

"Has your water broke?"

Rosalia shook her head.

"Has anyone been in here to take care of you?"

"A neighbor —" She took in several deep breaths. "But she hasn't come yet today.

This was too soon, Emily thought. Snake said she wasn't due for another month. She pulled the sheet back and was once again startled by how thin the woman was. "Have you been eating well?" Emily asked as she placed her hands over the enlarged belly. She felt movement beneath her fingertips, and blew out a deep sigh.

"A little. I haven't been able to keep much down."

Emily did a quick examination, then said, "Everything is looking good, you're already a little dilated. Your baby is definitely on its way."

"But it's too early," Rosalia protested.

Emily gave her a comforting smile. "It will be fine. Just relax and breathe. There you go," Emily said as she felt Rosalia start her deep breathing. She continued her examination, closing her eyes and concentrating on feeling the baby.

"I bet you haven't been out of this bed in a while. How about I take you for a little walk?"

"A walk?" Rosalia said, and looked confused.

"Yep. Come on," Emily said and helped Rosalia onto her feet. Then with one arm wrapped around her waist, they started for the door.

"Great timing," Peter said as they walked into the front room. "We need to get going."

"Rosalia shouldn't travel right now."

"Then we'll have to leave and send someone back for her. Baltasar has started a full-scale manhunt for us. We've already been here too long."

Rosalia flinched and a stricken look crossed her face.

Snake stepped forward. "I won't leave my sister."

"It's okay," Emily assured them. "Rosalia's in labor. We can't leave her to deliver on her own." As if to emphasize her words, another contraction surged through Rosalia and she nearly collapsed. Snake rushed forward to help Emily hold her up. She whispered in the poor woman's ear. "Breathe, Rosalia. You can do it."

Peter's shoulders dropped with acceptance. "All right. Tell us what we can do."

"Find me some clean blankets and towels and change the sheets on the bed. We're going to be in for a long day."

"You don't know the half of it," Peter muttered.

Emily knew Peter was worried, but she didn't see any alternative. They'd just have to hope Baltasar didn't find them. Either way, she couldn't abandon Rosalia and her child now. She'd already watched one child die; she would do everything she could for this one.

"Where are you going?" Snake asked as she helped Rosalia out the door.

"Just to get some fresh air and to walk around a bit out front. The movement will help get the labor progressing."

Snake nodded. "Okay, but don't go far and don't go into the jungle."

Emily stared at him. Was he kidding? "You don't have to worry about that. I don't plan on ever stepping foot into that jungle again." They left the hut and she walked Rosalia up and down the dirt road in front of a sprinkling of village houses. Women and children came out of their huts to ask if Rosalia was okay. A buzz of excitement filled the little street as children talked excitedly about the arrival of the new baby.

"Have you lived here long?" Emily asked Rosalia.

"No, only about six months. I used to live at Baltasar's estate," Rosalia said in between breaths.

Emily turned to her in surprise. "Really?"

"In one of the bungalows. Oh!" she gasped as another contraction hit her.

"It's okay. Just breathe. In and out, in and out."

As the contraction subsided they continued walking. "Baltasar and I were . . . friends," Rosalia admitted.

"Oh," Emily said, understanding.

"How is Marcos?" Rosalia asked.

Sadness filled Emily at the memory of the boy. She could still feel his little chest beneath her hands, as she tried to do Baltasar's bidding and bring the poor child back to life. It made her want to cry. "I'm afraid he passed on last night."

"Oh!" Rosalia said, at once distressed. She clutched her stomach. "I — I had hoped —"she shook her head without continuing the thought. "I cared for him very much. Like . . . like family." For a second, tears watered her eyes then she seemed to push them away.

"What happened," Emily asked, "between you and Baltasar?"

"He needed my help and I was foolish enough to cover for one of his mules —" she turned and explained "— women who deliver his drugs to his hotels around the world."

Emily nodded then stopped walking again as another contraction wracked Rosalia's small frame. They were coming faster now, faster and harder.

"Something happened and I got caught," she said on a shallow breath. "The drugs were confiscated. I managed to escape and since I was the only connection to tie the drugs back to Baltasar, I thought he'd be pleased."

"He wasn't?"

"No." She looked sad for a moment,

then the sadness turned to anger and something dark and hard glittered in her eyes. "It was like he'd lost his mind. He wasn't the same person. I don't know who he was." She looked away. "He beat me. Then he had that little creep Esteban beat me. I think he would have killed me, but Snake got me out and brought me here."

"He beat a pregnant woman?"

"He didn't know. I never told him, thank the Lord. It's a survivor, this little child of mine." She rubbed her stomach, and a smile crossed her face, before a convulsion of pain ripped through her again.

"Come on, let's get you back to the house," Emily said, not liking how hard and fast the contractions were coming.

"Don't let Baltasar find me or the baby. Promise me!" Her dark gaze bore into Emily and a shudder of fear shook her.

"Baltasar won't find any of us," Emily said with more conviction than she felt.

Rosalia nodded. The contractions and the worry were taking a toll on her — she looked exhausted. Suddenly, her water broke.

"Look's like it's time," Emily said and hurried her forward.

When they made their way back to the house and through the front door, Snake was ending a phone call. "I've checked with some contacts. Baltasar is less then thirty kilometers away. He'll be here in no time, so we need to leave now."

Emily stared at him horrified. "Rosalia's water just broke."

"I'm sorry. We have no choice."

Rosalia let loose a nerve-jarring scream and doubled over, clutching her stomach. "Quick, help me get her onto the bed," Emily demanded.

Snake picked up his sister and carried her into the back room. "We can't stay more than ten minutes," he urged.

"Pack lots of towels and blankets into the Jeep, and you'd better find us somewhere safe and clean to deliver this baby, because it's coming whether Baltasar's here or not."

Snake nodded and left the room. "And food," Emily yelled. "After the birth, we'll all be starving."

Rosalia screamed again. "It's coming."

Emily quickly examined her. To her immense relief, the baby was ready. "Okay, when I say, give a big push."

"Okay," Rosalia said, while struggling to breathe.

"You're doing great." Another contraction came. "Yes, now, push!"

Rosalia pushed with all her might, her face turning purple with the effort. A violent scream ripped through the house.

Snake opened the door and poked in his head. "Is everything okay?"

Emily turned to him. The poor man was ashen. "Yes, come here and help your sister push."

A look of horror crossed his face and he backed up a step.

"Come on, you can do it. Your sister needs you." And to think she'd been afraid of this man.

"What should I do?" he asked with a shaky voice.

"Hold her hand and encourage her to push, tell her she can do it, and help her to breathe."

He nodded, sat next to Rosalia's side, then took her hand and said something to her in Spanish. Rosalia looked up into her brother's face with such love, Emily couldn't help but smile.

Suddenly, Rosalia gasped and her stomach tightened as another contraction hit her. "Come on, Rosalia, push!"

Rosalia lifted herself up and pushed, screaming with the effort.

"There it is!" Emily said with excitement. "I can see its head. We're almost there."

Rosalia let out a deep breath and fell back against the bed, breathing heavily and trying to gather her strength, but Emily didn't like how tired she looked, how pale.

"Okay, honey, one more time," Emily said as she felt another contraction begin. As gently as she could, she held the baby's head and guided it as Rosalia pushed.

"The head is out now, Rosalia," Emily said, as she cradled the little head in her hand. Wonderment filled her as she stared at the tiny miracle. "Okay, Rosalia, one more big push!"

Rosalia screamed and pushed with all her might. The baby slid out of her thin, trembling body and into Emily's hands. She quickly wrapped it in a towel, cleaned out its nose and mouth, and rubbed its little back, then stared down into his beautiful little face and almost cried.

"It's a boy, Rosalia. A beautiful, perfect baby boy."

Rosalia's face sagged and she tried to catch her breath. Snake was rubbing her hand and grinning from ear to ear. "Did you hear that, Rosie? A boy."

Rosalia nodded, smiling as they hugged each other with joy. Emily continued to rub the baby's back and feet and soon it was inhaling its first lungful of air and crying.

Peter stuck his head in the door. Emily turned to him with tears shimmering in her eyes and showed him the baby still cradled in her arms. Peter's smile was small, and Emily realized he was worried about her. But she'd be fine. This baby was a miracle. Confirmation that God is good, and there is hope for a better world, a more loving world.

"I've heard word from your contacts," he said, looking at Snake. "Baltasar's almost here. I've informed the neighbors and asked them to evacuate the village."

"Can you give us a few more minutes? We're not quite done."

"It will be cutting it close."

"Please."

Her gaze met his for a long moment then he nodded. She quickly placed a clamp on the baby's umbilical cord, then handed Snake the scissors. He looked surprised, but gingerly did as she asked. Once the cord was cut, she handed Snake the baby. "Okay, Rosalia, I need just one more push, okay?"

Rosalia was limp but was doing her best. Still, Emily couldn't get the bleeding to stop and to top that off she didn't have time to suture the tears. Vigorously, she rubbed Rosalia's stomach, trying to get the uterus to clamp down and stop the bleeding.

"We're going to have to go and hope for the best," Snake said.

Emily sighed. "I guess we don't have a choice." She took the baby as Snake scooped his sister up, carried her outside and propped her up on a pile of towels in the back of the Jeep. Emily climbed in next to her then handed Rosalia her son.

"*Gracias,* Dr. Armstrong, for everything."

Emily smiled. "You did a good job, Mom. He's a beautiful baby boy."

Rosalia smiled at her baby and Emily wished, not for the first time, that they were safe in a hospital room and Rosalia was getting the care she needed. Instead, they were heading into the jungle in a Jeep that with each bounce and jiggle caused Rosalia an extreme amount of discomfort and pain.

"If you can, I need you to try and nurse your baby," Emily told her. "The sooner the better." Emily hoped that by nursing, Rosalia's body would produce enough oxytocin to slow or stop her bleeding.

Rosalia nodded, and though she was pale and tired, she did what she could. Snake drove down one dirt road after another speeding away from the village. In the passenger seat, Peter turned around looking behind them every now and then, his jaw tight, his muscles tense as if he expected to see Baltasar on their tail at any moment.

As he met Emily's gaze, she trembled at the stark concern in his eyes. It was much worse then when they were at the compound. Suddenly, she realized how much danger they were in and fear grew within her. They had to be okay. They couldn't have gone through all this and not be okay.

The bumping and jolting sent shafts of pain flashing across Rosalia's face. She clutched her child to her chest. Emily patted her arm and said a silent prayer. *Please, God, don't let Baltasar find us. Help us through this hard time. Help us escape this evil that threatens to hurt this innocent woman and her child. Let us all survive this day.*

Peter's face froze.

Following his gaze, Emily turned and looked behind her out the Jeep's back window. A cloud of black smoke rose above the trees and frightened birds flocked in the air, squawking in protest. Sounds carried and she heard shrieking that made her skin crawl. Her breath hung in her throat.

Rosalia gasped and, sensing her stress, her baby started to cry.

"What is it?" Emily asked, not wanting to hear the answer.

"Baltasar. He's burning the village."

Chapter Ten

Peter stared at the smoke rising in the distance and felt anger turn in his stomach. Baltasar was pure evil, and he needed to be stopped. That was why his work was so important, even if Emily couldn't see that. One day she'd have to.

Snake continued driving, without looking back, without flinching. Peter knew he had no choice. He had to save his sister and her child. There was nothing he could do for the people of the village now. He'd have to leave their fate up to the mercy of a madman, and to God.

After a while, Rosalia's cries in the back seat grew in intensity.

"Isn't there any way we can stop and let her rest?" Emily asked. "This bouncing is really hard on her."

Snake turned and looked at his sister, then looked at Emily. He pulled the Jeep off the road and into the jungle and turned off the engine. Peter wanted to say something, but the look of relief on Emily's and Rosalia's faces was so strong, he didn't have the heart. He and Snake got out while Emily checked Rosalia's bandages. "You feeling okay?" he heard Emily ask, but didn't hear Rosalia's reply.

He turned to Snake. "Isn't there anywhere safe we can leave the women?"

Snake stared at him, his gaze unreadable.

Peter didn't like asking, didn't like having to work with someone he didn't trust, and certainly didn't like being responsible for so many innocent lives. "We can't take two women and a newborn baby with us to the lab. Surely you must know someone we can leave them with?"

"It's too risky," Snake said.

"More risky than taking them with us?"

"The women aren't safe anywhere in Venezuela," Snake replied.

"Then what's your plan?" Peter hated the way the words sounded, hated having to ask Baltasar's number-one thug what they were going to do next. This was his mission, Emily was his problem, but the worst part was that right now he didn't see any other alternative.

"Once we're in Colombia, it will be easier to get them to America."

"What about the lab?"

Snake rubbed the stubble on his jaw. "There's a village I know — friends I trust

— fifteen miles on this side of the border. We can leave them there then I'll take you to the lab. You do what you need to, then I'll do what I need to for Rosalia and Dr. Armstrong."

"You can leave Dr. Armstrong to me," Peter said, not liking the way Snake was taking claim to Emily.

Snake raised his eyebrows, but didn't ask. Which was good, because Peter wasn't about to explain.

Emily climbed out of the Jeep. Her face was drawn and she was wiping blood off her hands and onto a towel.

"How's Rosalia?" Snake asked.

"The bleeding is slowing, but all this bouncing around is not helping. Her body needs time to heal."

Snake nodded. "I'll see what I can do."

Peter stepped toward her and held out his hand. "Let's go for a walk."

"Don't go far," Snake muttered.

"Wouldn't dream of it," Peter responded. "How is Rosalia, really?" he asked Emily once they moved away from the Jeep. He could see the concern in her eyes. It was what made her such a good doctor, her ability to care about anybody, even perfect strangers, when she should be caring about herself.

"Not good, I'm afraid. We really need to get her to a hospital."

Peter agreed. "We need to get you both out of here as quickly as we can."

"I understand that, but can we just rest here for thirty minutes?"

Peter hesitated. "Let's sit down." He led her into a private clearing, and they sat on a fallen log. He felt a pinch on his arm, and immediately wiped away a large insect. Without some form of bug repellent, they were going to get eaten alive.

"She really needs it."

"All right," he relented. He had no choice in the matter. It wasn't his Jeep, and it looked as if Snake had taken control of his mission.

"Thanks, Peter. She's had a real tough time." She filled him in on what Rosalia had told her about Baltasar. "Why do you think Snake continued to work for Baltasar after that?"

"I can't imagine," Peter said dryly. There were a lot of things about Snake he just couldn't put his finger on. "See what you can find out from Rosalia."

She stiffened. "Peter, we all had a rough night and an even tougher morning. Please don't tell me to start prying into other people's lives."

This was so typical of Emily, trying to force him into a defensive position. "The last thing in the world I would want is to tell you what to do, Emily. Even if you do owe me."

"Owe you? How can you say that? I saw that plane barreling down the runway and I thought you left me. I had no choice but to go with Snake."

Surprise choked him. "How could you think I left you? I defied orders twice to come back for you."

"You did?" It was her turn to look surprised. "You put *me* before your job?"

"I'll be lucky if I still have a job after we get out of this."

"Really?" A grin of immense pleasure covered her face.

"Don't look so happy."

She tried to force a serious expression on her face, but the smile kept poking through. "Okay, I won't."

He shook his head and couldn't help the grin teasing the corners of his mouth. She had to be the most exasperating woman ever born. He'd come halfway around the world to get away from her and here she was messing up his life like some huge cosmic joke.

"I am glad you came back for me," she

admitted. "Even if we did miss the plane."

"I could never leave your life in someone else's hands," he muttered, even if he really, really wanted to.

"I guess it's good for me that you like being in charge and handling things on your own."

"You're right, I do, and I definitely don't like working with Snake."

"He's not so bad."

He looked at her sharply. "What was *that* supposed to mean?"

She grinned. "Compared to you, that is."

He knew he shouldn't, but he wrapped his hand in her hair and pulled her to him. "Stop looking at me like that," he said, his lips mere inches from hers.

"Like what?" Her large luminous eyes bore directly into his.

"With that sparkle on your face. I don't like it."

"You don't?" She pouted, her bottom lip sticking out, looking even more luscious, even more desirable than he remembered seeing it. He knew it was a mistake, a colossal mistake, like many others he'd made since he first saw her in Baltasar's office, but he just couldn't stop himself.

He pressed his lips against hers and kissed her with everything he had, and all he'd missed during the last three years he'd spent in the jungle. His lips moved against hers and he was filled with longing for her touch, for her smile at breakfast in the morning, for her arms wrapped around him at night as they drifted off to sleep. He was filled with her — his wife, his love.

He pulled away. He had to stop. She looked at him questioningly, her aching vulnerability shining in her eyes. He just let her believe they had a chance, a future. Now he'd have to disappoint her all over again. "I was so afraid something had happened to you," he said. It was true, but it was also a feeble excuse for his inability to control himself around her.

She ran a finger across her swollen lips, and smiled. "I'm pretty good at taking care of myself."

"Really?" he said.

"You don't believe me?"

"You are a disaster waiting to happen."

"Ha!" She smacked his arm. "You are in serious trouble now."

He looked at her with mock horror. "Please don't hurt me."

"You'd better watch it, buddy, or I'll give you a little taste of what I gave to Esteban."

A twinge of anxiety poked him. "You messed with Esteban?"

"Let's put it this way. I think Esteban will think twice the next time he tries to mess with me."

Peter tried to hold back the laugh rising in his throat. She couldn't be serious.

"You don't believe me?"

"I never doubt you," he said, and the moment the words left his mouth he knew they were a lie. He did doubt her. All the time. He doubted she'd ever be able to put her fears behind her and trust what they had. He doubted she'd be able to commit her whole heart to him, because she'd always keep a little back in reserve in case he got hurt again, in case he didn't come back home. And that little bit of her heart that she kept from him would be all she needed to convince herself to leave him.

And he couldn't go through that again.

He stood, he couldn't do this anymore.

"Peter, wait." She placed her hand on his arm.

He looked down at it.

"I'm sorry for all the trouble I've given you."

He looked into her eyes, trying to gauge her level of sincerity.

"I know I should have taken my chances with the motorcycle. I should have left with you and Robert. My stubbornness has put us all in this terrible situation."

"Emily, if you had gone over the wall or had gotten on that plane, then Rosalia and her baby could have died."

Emily nodded, her face grim.

She knew what he was saying; he could see it in her eyes. He took a deep breath and continued. "I have to believe that God wanted you here to save them, otherwise, why would all this have happened?"

"Do you really believe that?"

"Why do you look so surprised?"

She turned away, sadness and guilt heavy in her expression.

He took her by the chin, and turned her back to him. "What is it?"

"After the explosion, when you were in the hospital, I promised God if He let you live, I'd never leave you, that I'd be the best wife ever."

His breath caught in his chest. He vaguely remembered hearing her voice as she sat by his hospital bed, pleading to God to let him live. He *had* lived. Only she hadn't stayed. The memory clutched his heart in its icy grasp. As soon as she found out he'd be okay, she walked out of his life and never turned back.

"I obviously broke that promise," she said with a catch in her voice.

He didn't say anything, couldn't trust himself not to sound angry or bitter.

"I was too afraid you'd go back out and do it again. I'm sorry, Peter." Her eyes misted with tears. He stared at the ground beneath his feet and concentrated on the giant ants moving around on the jungle floor.

"I've had a hard time forgiving myself for that decision."

He could only imagine.

"And worse, I let myself believe that God hadn't forgiven me, either."

He looked at her in surprise. "God doesn't hold grudges, people do."

"I know, but I guess it was easier to believe that than to think about it too much. I gave up on us and I gave up on God. It wasn't until I've been here that I've allowed myself to open up to Him again. To hope that maybe He has forgiven me."

"Seek the Lord and you will find Him if you look for Him with all your heart and soul."

She smiled. "Marcos helped tear down the wall I'd built around my heart."

He couldn't help feeling surprised as he listened to her. She'd never been this honest with him before. Maybe she had changed.

"I only knew him for a short time, but he

was such a special child. Even after all he'd been through, he loved without fear, without holding back."

"The innocence of babes."

She smiled. "Baltasar was so lucky to have him. I hope he realized that." She paused. "I'd have given anything to have a child like him. To have your child."

A heavy silence lay between them. It wasn't anything he hadn't heard before, but this time things were different. This was a road they would never be able to take. Not anymore. Not since the explosion had left him unable to father a child. "I'm sorry, Em."

"Me, too." She sighed. "But I've learned something about myself through all this. I don't like people telling me what to do. I don't like other people deciding things for me. And I really don't like my total lack of control over the decisions you make, and the tremendous effect those decisions have over my life. In other words, I don't like the chances you take."

"And that's a new revelation?"

"No, but I've learned that I don't have enough trust, either. Trust that you're good enough at your job to come home safe, or trust that you'll put me first above your job."

"Haven't I just proved that to you?"

"Yeah," she smiled. "I guess you have."

"Em, I don't see how any of this can change things between us. Our lives have gone in different directions."

"No, your life has taken the turn, not mine. I'm still sitting at home waiting for you to come back. I just hadn't realized it."

"I don't think I can."

She touched his hand. "Peter . . ."

"Shh. Let's not talk about it, not anymore today."

"Just promise me you'll think about it." She looked up at him with such hope and promise in her eyes, it was all he could do not to pull her into his arms and offer her the moon. In some ways he supposed that would be easier than giving her back his heart.

She wrapped her arms around him and snuggled up close. And while Peter relished the feel of her against him, he knew it could only be temporary. As soon as he got the information he needed from the lab, he'd get her safely tucked back in Colorado Springs. Then he'd be off again, to parts unknown on some new mission, under some new name. He had to, it was his only choice. Because regardless of what they still meant to each other, there were still too many reasons that kept them apart.

After they'd rested and eaten, they traveled the remainder of the day then stopped for the night. Snake removed two small tents from the back of the Jeep and a few blankets. Emily stared at the tents that looked barely big enough for one, let alone two, and wondered if Peter would join her in the tent or sleep with Snake in the Jeep. She'd opened her heart to him and had hoped he could see how sorry she was — she'd hoped he'd be able to forgive her.

She pushed the disappointment out of her mind. She needed to let herself trust Peter to do what was right by her, and she needed to put her faith back in God. If they were supposed to be together then she would have to trust God to bring him back to her. To keep them safe. She jumped as some creature screamed in the night. Easier said than done, she realized.

She crawled into the small tent and thought about what Peter had said about seeking the Lord and finding him. Deep down in her heart she knew his words were true. She knew that's what she had to do.

She closed her eyes and prayed, asking God to forgive her for her broken promises, and for all the mistakes she'd made and all the ones she'd make in the future. Because she wasn't perfect and she was still learning, and still hoping that she'd be able to give her heart completely to God and to Peter, and to trust that they would both be there for her. It was a huge leap of faith, but one she wanted with all her heart to take.

"Please Lord, watch after us this night, and keep a special eye on Rosalia and her sweet baby." As the child entered her mind, a bittersweet ache filled her. He was so small and precious. She'd never forget the joy that filled her the instant he came into the world. He was everything she had always wished for. And more. "Someday, Lord, please give Peter and I a child of our own. It's what I long for, what I want more than anything in the world."

The next morning, she sat up and listened for the sound of Peter's voice, suddenly afraid that something had happened to him, that Baltasar had found them. She heard him talking softly to Snake and relief filled her. She sighed; somehow they'd have to find a way to make it safely through another day.

She climbed out of the tent and checked on Rosalia and her baby.

"How is she doing?" Snake asked.

"A little better. She's healing and the

bleeding has slowed, but I'm afraid she's getting an infection."

"Is there anything you can do?"

"Not without antibiotics. We'll have to get her to a hospital as soon as we can."

Snake nodded. They had a quick meal from the few items that Snake had brought, then Rosalia fed her baby. Emily couldn't help smiling as she watched the baby nursing. "He's such a good baby. He didn't even wake me last night."

"He fed three times," Rosalia said proudly.

"Have you decided on a name?"

"I'm going to call him Manuel after my father." Snake's face broke into a pleased grin.

"That's a wonderful name," Emily said.

Peter sat next to her. "You about ready?"

She didn't think she could ever be ready to face what this day would bring. She plastered a grin on her face and said, "Bring it on."

Chapter Eleven

Four hours later, Emily leaned back in the seat and closed her eyes. She hated the jungle. From her small window in the back of the Jeep, she found herself peering through the dense foliage. She saw something large moving through the trees, but couldn't tell what it was, or if it presented a threat. But she was thankful they were in a vehicle, and though it wasn't moving fast, it was obviously moving fast enough.

She was tired of feeling afraid. She felt raw, emotionally and physically. She'd been here too long, felt too many extreme emotions from hope to fear to heartache. Everything was too real here, too harsh.

Rosalia had been quiet too long and Emily didn't care for the fine sheen covering her skin or the pallor of her face. "Are you feeling okay, Rosalia?"

"*Sí, señorita.* I'm just hot."

"Me, too." This jungle was a miserable place — hot, sticky, buggy. She had bites on her bites. What she wouldn't give to be back in Colorado Springs. "How much farther until we get there?" she asked, growing impatient.

"Soon," Snake said. "I'm taking you to the village of a friend of mine and Rosalia's." He said something in Spanish and Rosalia nodded, smiling. "We'll have lunch, then I'm going to leave you three there while Peter and I check out the lab."

Emily nodded. She didn't like the idea of being left in a strange village with people she didn't know, but she'd rather be there than at Baltasar's lab. She didn't want to be anywhere near that man or anything of his ever again.

"We should be back by nightfall," Peter added.

"What if you're not?" Emily asked.

"Then my friend will get you and Rosalia to a hospital in Colombia," Snake said.

"But we will be back. Trust that, Em. Snake and I —" Peter looked at Snake "— we're both real good at what we do. We won't take any unnecessary risks."

"Promise?" she asked.

"*Sí,*" they both said in unison.

Emily smiled. "You two are starting to sound like partners."

"Bite your tongue," Peter mumbled, and turned to look out his window.

Emily sighed. Another day and this whole nightmare would be over. She looked up in expectation as signs of a village nestled among the trees and vines came into view. Chickens and children and an occasional pig roamed the street. Enchanted by the scene and anxious to get out of the Jeep, Emily opened the door as soon as the vehicle pulled to a stop in a clearing in front of a row of small huts.

One of the children came forward. He was smiling and appeared to be excited by their presence. "Are you an American?" he asked, in halting English.

Emily nodded. "I am. What is your name?"

He smiled shyly. "Carlos."

"Hello, Carlos." Emily turned and watched Snake help Rosalia, with her arms around Manuel, out of the Jeep and walk her toward a small thatched house. Peter, too, got out and stretched his long arms toward the sky. He looked over at her talking to the boy and smiled, a devastatingly handsome smile that took firm hold of her heart and gave it a fierce tug.

"Are you the lady doctor?" Carlos asked.

Emily turned back to him. "Yes, how did you know that?"

A troubled look came over his face as if

he'd said something he shouldn't have and suddenly Emily knew how he knew. Fear slammed into her. She turned, and from the corner of her eye saw a man in a Jeep parked just off the road hidden in the trees.

"Peter!" she screamed, and it seemed as though her voice echoed through the trees, reverberating through the jungle. Peter turned, but it was too late. The man was standing, holding some kind of huge weapon on his shoulder. A big grin split his dirty brown face. The world stopped as she watched him fire the device. Something shot through the air and impacted with the Jeep, lifting it off the ground.

The Jeep exploded into a huge fireball. A wave of heat knocked her off her feet and sent her flying. She hit the ground hard, tumbling end over end. She heard the boy screaming, and tried to find him through the thick smoke. Glass and chunks of burning metal fell all around her. She spotted him and crawled over the boy, then curled up into a ball, and covered him with her body, trying to protect him as well as she could.

Stars swam before her eyes. Acrid smoke filled her nose. She lay there for a minute trying to comprehend what happened, trying to determine how badly hurt she was, but everything ached, and a high-pitched sound rang through her ears. The boy was silently weeping. "Are you okay?" she asked. She looked him over, but other than a few bumps and scratches, he appeared to be fine. He glanced behind her, his eyes growing wide, then he jumped up and ran away.

What had he seen?

She was afraid to look. She could feel the heat from the burning Jeep at her back, could hear the screams and panic of the villagers as they ran out of their homes and disappeared into the jungle.

But she did look. She forced herself to turn and stare at the burning wreckage of their vehicle. Emotion overwhelmed her.

Peter.

Her stomach turned. She couldn't think, couldn't stand, couldn't find the strength to approach the Jeep and prove to herself that Peter was safe. That, by some miracle of God, he had survived the explosion.

Suddenly, shots were being fired. She looked back and saw Snake running toward her. The man with the dirty face had dropped the gun that was big enough to blow up Jeeps and was pointing a rifle directly at her. "No!" she cried, but she couldn't seem to make herself move.

As if stuck in a dream, she watched Snake stop and level his gun, firing a direct hit. The man collapsed to his knees. Crimson blood saturated his shirt, then he hit the ground face first, falling on the gun. The next thing she knew, Snake had her by the waist, was lifting her up and pulling her toward the burning Jeep.

"No," she cried. "I can't . . . Peter." She couldn't see him like that. God help her, she couldn't handle it.

They rounded the burning vehicle; about twenty feet away Peter was lying on the ground, his big blue eyes looking directly at her.

"Oh, Peter!" She ran to his side and dropped to her knees. "How'd you get away?"

He gave her a goofy smile. "Saw it coming, jumped."

Relieved laughter bubbled in her throat. She turned to Snake as tears slid down her cheek. "He jumped."

Snake's eyes narrowed.

Emily turned back to Peter. His eyes drifted closed and his head flopped to one side. Fear and hopelessness grabbed hold of her heart and, for a moment, she felt dizzy with it. *Oh, God, no.* Peter's hand fell away from his shoulder, and she could see blood soaking through his shirt and running down his chest. A large piece of twisted metal stuck out of his shoulder.

Emily gritted her teeth. She knew what she had to do. With trembling fingers, she reached for the metal.

Snake crouched next to her. "Your bag was in the Jeep, along with the phone, food and all our supplies."

"Can you find me anything? Water? Bandages? Towels?" She tried to sound calm and professional, but at the moment it was taking all the control she had not to break down and collapse. Snake nodded and ran toward the small thatched houses. Emily focused on the metal and tried not to think about the fact that this was Peter's shoulder, Peter's blood all over her hands.

Gently, she eased the metal out of his shoulder.

"Hey," Peter yelled, coming to.

She quickly applied pressure over the wound to stop the bleeding.

Snake came running up carrying bandages, towels, water and whiskey. Before Emily could say a word, he poured the alcohol over Peter's wound.

Peter howled in protest. Emily shoved gauze against the wound and taped it to his skin. She placed a towel over it and brought Peter's hand to the wound. "Apply constant pressure."

He stared at it and nodded.

"We have to go," Snake said. "News of this will get out and others will be coming soon."

"But how?" Emily said, and gestured toward their burning Jeep.

Peter nodded toward the attacker's Jeep. "We'll just have to borrow his. It doesn't look like he'll need it."

Emily had to agree with that. "What about Rosalia? Are you going to leave her here with your friends?"

"My friend was gone. His wife and daughters, too."

Emily was afraid to ask. "Not dead?"

"No."

But Emily could read the concern in his eyes. Before she could comment further, Snake put an arm under Peter's shoulder and lifted him up. Peter winced, but stood. After they got him settled in the front of the Jeep, she picked up the massive gun that had done so much damage and got ready to heft it into the jungle.

"Hey, that's a grenade launcher. Bring that over here," Peter protested.

"You're not serious."

"Absolutely. And get his rifle, too."

"But he's holding it."

"So?"

Emily looked at the man lying in the dirt. "He's dead."

"I hope so. I wouldn't ask you to pry it out of his hands if he wasn't."

Emily shuddered. "We'll wait for Snake to do that."

"Suit yourself." Peter leaned back against the seat and closed his eyes.

Snake and Rosalia came hurrying up as fast as they could. Emily held the baby and helped her into the Jeep, while Snake retrieved the rifle. Within minutes, they were on the road again, traveling as fast as they could through the jungle. Emily sighed and settled back into the seat. "Looks like we're going with you to the lab," she muttered.

"Let's just hope we make it there before Baltasar discovers what happened," Snake said.

"Why's that?"

"It would be better if he didn't find out how close we are to his lab, or he'll be waiting for us when we get there."

Emily had a feeling he'd be waiting for them anyway. They hadn't traveled very long, perhaps forty-five minutes or an hour, when the Jeep began to sputter. "What is it?" she asked, not liking the sound one bit.

"We're running out of gas," Snake muttered.

Emily looked at the dense jungle around them. "Don't say that." *Don't even think that.*

He let the Jeep drift to a stop.

"What are we going to do?" Emily groaned.

"Hold on and I'll check the jerry can." Snake got out of the Jeep and walked around back. He unlatched the large red gas can and shook it. Then he threw it against the ground.

Emily jumped.

"It's dry," he grumbled.

"How can it be dry? It's not like there are gas stations in the jungle. What was that man thinking?"

"Obviously he wasn't planning on going far."

"Either that or he planned to get gas from someone in the village." Emily got out and walked around the Jeep to Peter's side and opened the door. He was sleeping soundly. She gave him a gentle shake. "Peter, wake up."

"What is it?"

"We're out of gas. We have to go back to the village to get more."

"What?" Peter climbed out of the Jeep. "How long have we been driving?"

"Not long enough," Snake said. "There's still a good ten miles until we reach the lab."

Ten miles. The bottom dropped out of Emily's stomach.

"We're going to have to walk," Snake said, and grabbed some gear out of the back of the Jeep.

"Rosalia and I will wait here with the baby," Emily said practically.

Snake's eyebrows rose in surprise. "We're all going together."

Outraged, Emily turned to Peter. He shrugged, winced, and then checked his bandage. "The bleeding's stopped."

"We can't go with you!" Emily protested and stared back down the pothole-ridden dirt road they had just traveled.

"If you stay here, there's a good chance you'll be shot to death. Which do you prefer?"

Emily stared at him while his words sunk in. "All right," she relented, but she didn't understand why they all needed to trudge back to the village just to get gas. She turned to help Rosalia out of the Jeep. The poor woman looked exhausted. "Come on, Rosalia. It's not too far."

Snake pushed the Jeep off the road and through some trees, then continued up the road.

"Hey, where are you going?" Emily demanded. "The village is that way." She gestured behind them.

"There is no one there that can or will help us. No one goes against *El Patrón*."

"But surely you can get more gas there, or even another Jeep?"

"Don't count on it. Besides, by the time we'd get there the place would be swarming with opportunists wanting to wipe out the American lady doctor who killed *El Patrón*'s son."

Emily blanched. "Surely you don't mean that we're going to walk the rest of the way to Colombia through the jungle?"

Snake didn't answer. Didn't even turn to look.

"Peter!" She was shrieking. She could hear it in her tone. But she didn't care.

"Sorry, Em," Peter said, as he trailed after Snake. "We've got to get to the lab. Trust me, we want to get there before nightfall."

"Lady, you can do whatever you want," Snake called. "Pietro and I have an arrangement, and if that means walking the next ten miles through the jungle to do it, then that's what we're going to do. Take it or leave it."

And here she actually thought she was beginning to like that man.

"As if I have any choice," she yelled back.

"You don't. So if you don't mind zipping it, I'd appreciate it."

"Oh, gee thanks. Consider me zipped," Emily grumbled as she trailed farther behind them. She couldn't get over him. Over Peter! Bewilderment filled her as she stared at him. Wasn't he just lying on the ground bleeding all over the place? Now he wanted to walk ten miles through the jungle. Surely there must be a better way. But as she stared at him, she realized that even without his long hair he looked right at home here in the jungle. In fact, he looked to be in his element.

Emily turned away. He certainly didn't look like a man who would be happy picking up the kids at preschool and living a mundane, boring life back in Colorado Springs. He looked like this was his life now — this dark and dangerous jungle. Who was Peter Vance, anyway? Because this man striding down the road in front of her bore no resemblance to her ex-husband.

She trudged after them, looking left, then right, peering into the dense foliage, trying not to think about the multitudes of beady eyes staring out at her from the dark green leaves. What if they didn't make it to the lab by nightfall? Where would they sleep? The tents burned up in the Jeep with everything else. She couldn't survive a night in the jungle without a tent. Without shelter. Without water or bug spray or anything.

Hysteria swelled within her.

"Come on, Dr. Armstrong," Rosalia said, taking her arm. "It will be okay. Trust my brother. He grew up in this jungle. He won't let anything happen to us."

Emily turned to her, surprised by her determination, and equally surprised by how hot and clammy her skin was. "Rosalia, are you okay? You feel like you're running a fever."

"A slight one. It will be okay."

Admiration filled her as she watched Rosalia walk down the uneven road with her child. She knew every step was painful for her, yet the woman showed no sign of weakness or distress. "You're right. We're going to be just fine." *As soon as we get you both to a hospital where you belong,* Emily thought silently.

Chapter Twelve

After an hour of walking through the heat, they were blessed with a rainstorm. At least Emily thought it was a blessing as the sudden downpour washed the dust and the muck off of her skin. But once the rain stopped, the moisture seemed to evaporate, leaving the air thick and heavy. She couldn't breathe, and to top it off, she was sloshing through mud.

"Please," she groaned. "Isn't there somewhere, anywhere that Rosalia and I can stay? I don't think Rosalia can take much more of this," Emily said, then cringed as she stepped into a particularly deep puddle and felt a painful jarring in her back as muddy water sloshed into her socks. "Or me for that matter."

The men, trudging quite a ways ahead of her, kept going. Her arms itched and stung. She swiped her hand down her skin and wiped off fifty or so mosquitoes taking a drink. She didn't think she was going to make it. Not another step. She glanced down and saw . . . *blood*.

She stopped, staring at the blood seeping

through her wet, muddy sock. "Oh, no!" she cried. She clawed at her sock, pulling it out from against her skin, and stared at a leech stuck to her foot. A horrified scream ripped from her insides and echoed through the jungle.

She dropped to the muddy ground and ripped her shoes and socks off, trying to get it off her skin. Tears filled her eyes and rolled down her cheeks. Then Peter was in front of her, bending down, prying the giant black slug-looking thing off of her. A large wound bled copiously. Emily stared at her foot in shocked disbelief.

"It was only a leech," Peter said casually, as if it were nothing at all. As if leeches were a normal part of everyday life. Not her life! "Be thankful it wasn't a tick. Those little buggers are nasty."

And these aren't? Emily ground her teeth. She couldn't trust herself to speak. If she did, she would most likely come unglued and start screaming hysterically before it died down to an incoherent babble.

"You'll be fine. It will just itch like crazy for a few days."

Emily stared at him. Every inch of her body was aching and swollen and he acted like it was no big deal — just a little itch. What about the trauma? The nightmares she was sure to suffer? Because she was certain she would never be able to close her eyes again without seeing that thing attached to her.

"Em?"

She opened her mouth to respond, but her voice was gone, her will was gone, and suddenly she wondered how she would be able to make it the rest of the way when all she wanted to do was sit there and cry and wait for someone to come rescue her. She couldn't take any more. She had reached her limit.

He stood and held out his hand to her. She stared at it, but she wouldn't take it. She wasn't moving. She turned away from him. He would have to send a helicopter back for her and Rosalia because she refused to take another step.

"Emily, it's not a good idea to sit in the mud, unless you want a leech down your pants."

She shot up, and started swatting at her bottom and running her hands inside the waistband of her jeans, tears of frustration once again welling in her eyes. "I can't do this. I can't take any more."

"Sure you can. You're tougher than you think."

"No, I'm not."

"Yes, you are." He placed his arm around her shoulder and led her forward to meet up with Rosalia and Snake. "You can do anything you set your mind to, Dr. Armstrong."

She had always believed that, even after her parents died and she had to force herself to go to class, to turn in her assignments, to graduate. Until now. She leaned against him and closed her eyes, letting him lead her, not wanting to see the endless jungle in front of and surrounding her. She'd been such a fool to come to Venezuela. She cursed the day she ever decided to leave her nice apartment with her comfortable bed and hot shower. She thought of that shower now, imagined the hot spray of water and the lavender scent of her favorite exfoliating soap. What she wouldn't give to be back home now.

"Dr. Armstrong," Snake called.

Reluctantly, Emily opened her eyes. Snake was holding Rosalia to keep her from collapsing. "Oh, no!" She ran toward them, feeling guilty for her self-pitying tirade, when Rosalia was in real trouble, serious trouble.

Rosalia's eyes were closed, and her skin was clammy and pale. "Rosalia?"

A soft moan escaped her parted lips.

Emily felt her head. "She needs antibiotics," she said, but they all knew she needed so much more. Snake opened Rosalia's shirt and removed Manuel from the sling they'd fashioned, then handed Emily the baby. Peter unbuttoned his shirt and slid it over her shoulders. He buttoned up the baby in the fabric so he was completely covered. Snake lifted his sister into his arms, whispering to her in Spanish, and continued walking through the jungle.

"We have to get her to a hospital immediately," Emily whispered to Peter. "If we don't . . ."

He turned to her and nodded his head, his expression stopping her from saying the words. He knew how serious it was. It was clear what would happen to all of them if they didn't get out of Venezuela soon. Unfortunately they still had miles and miles of jungle to trek through.

Emily shuddered as despair wracked her. She stared at the exposed wound on Peter's shoulder. The wound that needed stitches, the wound that could easily become infected, too. Especially since they were walking though a cesspool of foreign and deadly bacteria.

"I don't think finding this lab is a good

idea, Peter. I think our top priority needs to be finding a hospital."

He nodded. "To do that, we need to get to the lab."

"Peter, who knows what we'd be walking into? You and Rosalia can't take any more chances."

"Emily, I need to fulfill my mission. That's why I'm here."

A dark cloud surrounded her. Who was this man? How could he put some stupid mission above their safety? Why did the "mission" always come first? "What is wrong with you? Don't you see how desperate our situation has become? Can't you see what's at stake here?"

He stopped and turned to her. "I would never have been able to survive in this jungle for the last three years if I didn't keep my eye on the ball. We will find the lab, we will find a phone, we will find a Jeep and water, food and medical supplies, and then we will get all of us to a hospital. You have to learn to trust me, Emily."

He was right. "All right," she relented. "I trust you. I do," she insisted. But the look in his eyes told her he didn't believe her. And she supposed on some level he was right.

Inside Peter's shirt, the baby began to

squirm against her breasts. The poor thing must be hungry. She peeked inside her shirt. "Sorry, fella," she whispered. "I can't help you."

He looked up at her and his big brown eyes filled her with tenderness. "Hi," she whispered, and smiled. "How you doing in there?" She looked up and caught Peter staring at her, but it wasn't a warm, loving look. It was cold and wary. Then, like a wave of sadness washing over her body, the certain knowledge that they would never have a child together hit her. It was as clear as the regret shining in his eyes.

She turned away from him. As they walked, Snake and Peter took turns carrying Rosalia. At one point they stopped to rest, Peter and Snake needing it as much as she did. While Rosalia fed her baby, Emily noticed the blood seeping through Peter's bandage. As thin and small as she was, Rosalia's weight was too much for his injured shoulder. She thought of the other woman's open wound and the infection raging through her body.

And if the same thing happened to Peter?

She couldn't think on it, there was nothing she could do, no one she could turn to except for God. She closed her eyes and prayed, the heartfelt motion coming easily to her, as if it hadn't been such a struggle for her during the three years before she came to Venezuela.

Dear God, please look out for us. Please let us all make it to the hospital safely, and whatever You do, please don't let Peter get sick.

Without saying a word, she leaned forward and applied pressure to Peter's wound until the bleeding stopped. She didn't know how she would find the strength to fight her way out of Venezuela if Peter got sick. The fear came rushing back, the way it always had every time he'd walked out their front door. In the end, she hadn't been able to deal with it. She'd forgotten how strong it was, how forceful that fear could be.

She'd actually thought she'd be able to live with it again. That if she could just get him to forgive her and come back things would be different this time, but she'd been wrong. Maybe that was why God had put her on this path. Maybe she needed to see the truth before she could move on. The Lord knew she hadn't been able to move on, because she hadn't been able to let Peter go.

Is that it, God? Is that why we're going

*through this nightmare? So that I can fi-
nally see that this is where Peter belongs?
This is his life, and I can never be a part of
it? Wouldn't a two-by-four across the side
of the head have been easier?*

She was such an idiot.

*All right, God, I've learned my lesson. I
get it. There's no future for Peter and me,
no chance for a happily-ever-after, for a
child.* She looked down at baby Manuel
and swallowed the bitter taste in her
mouth. There was no chance they could
be a family again. The force of unfulfilled
and lost dreams hit her. She had to let
Peter go. She had to move on. She tried
not to look at him, and tried even harder
not to cry.

They all rose and started walking again,
but Rosalia was growing significantly
worse, and Emily feared if they didn't get
to a hospital soon, the young mother
wouldn't make it.

"Please," she said to Snake and Peter.
"This isn't working. You two can move
faster without us. At this point, Rosalia
needs to save her strength."

Snake shook his head. "There is too
much danger for you if you stop moving.
We must stay together. Our only hope is to
make it to the lab and find a Jeep there.

230

Then we can cross the border and find a hospital in Colombia."

Emily shook her head in defeat. She knew Snake loved his sister, and if he thought that was their only course of action, then she'd have to trust that he was right, and trust that God wouldn't let them perish in this horrible jungle.

But most of all, she'd have to hope that Baltasar wasn't waiting for them at the lab when they got there.

Peter slowed as Emily trailed farther behind them. He knew how frustrating it must be for her to watch her patient grow worse and worse, and not be able to do anything to help. He only hoped they were right, and that they would find a vehicle or at least a phone at Baltasar's lab.

The baby started to cry. He watched Emily try to calm it. It pained him to see how good she looked with a baby in her arms. She would make a wonderful mother. He wished he could be a part of that picture, but even if they could get past all their problems and issues with the past, he could never impose his lifestyle on a child. His father had done that and it had been hard on all of them, never knowing where his dad was or when he'd come home. The all-too-frequent business trips and the loneliness they saw in their mother's eyes was too much.

Once he and Emily divorced, he'd become an undercover operative. It had been his choice, and one he wouldn't go back on. He was good at what he did. He was needed. It was his life now.

A wide muddy river came into view ahead of them. They stopped at the edge of the road and stared at the bridge that had collapsed into the water. Peter's stomach dropped. He fought the despair that suddenly everything was going wrong. That he kept missing the mark.

First he botched the mission at the estate, then he botched Emily's rescue by not demanding that she come with him and Dr. Fletcher, and they almost got themselves blown up because Baltasar obviously knew right where they were heading. And now someone had destroyed the bridge they needed to cross to get to the lab. It was as if Baltasar was one step ahead of their every move.

Peter glanced at Snake. Was he leading them into a trap? Was Rosalia really his sister? Why hadn't that man shot at the Jeep while they were still in it? It was almost as if he hadn't wanted them dead. It was almost as if Baltasar wanted them wounded and struggling, but alive.

Peter didn't like the road his thoughts were taking. He watched Snake, trying to get a handle on the man who seemed to have no allegiances. Why hadn't Snake questioned him about why Emily kept calling him Peter, and how it was they apparently knew each other so well? Did he already know Peter was CIA? Did he already know their history?

Something wasn't right.

"What happened to the bridge?" Emily cried.

"Rain could have washed it away," Snake offered.

"Or Baltasar," Peter said, and tried to read Snake's expression as he turned back to him.

"We'll go around," Snake said.

"To where?" Emily questioned. "This river looks like it goes on for miles."

"To the next bridge."

"How far is that?" she demanded.

Peter smiled inwardly. She was beginning to lose her temper, and he had a feeling that would work best for their position at the moment. He'd been too quick to give control to Snake. He'd put their lives in this man's hands, a man they knew nothing about. It was time to take back the reins of his mission.

"How far are we from the lab now?" Peter asked casually.

"Two miles, if we could cross the bridge here."

"How many more if we walk up to the next bridge?" Emily demanded.

"Another five on top of that."

"No," she insisted. "There is no way I'm walking another five miles. For one thing it will be dark before we get there, and you're not going to get me to walk around in the dark. For another thing, Rosalia —" she started and looked at Peter as if by the will of that look alone she could force him to do whatever she demanded. He tried not to smile. "Those extra miles would be too much for her."

"Then what do you suggest?" Snake asked, his eyes narrowing, but his question had opened the door wide open.

"I say we swim," Emily responded. "How deep is it?"

"With the baby?" Snake sputtered.

"Well . . . how deep is it?" she demanded.

"I have no idea."

"We don't have to swim far, just to the bridge. If we can climb up onto the bridge, we can walk the rest of the way."

Snake stared at the bridge. "It's impossible to tell how stable that bridge is. It could collapse beneath us, then what would we do? We'd be carried downstream and Rosalia and her baby will die. I'm not going to chance it."

"Fine. You walk up to the nearest bridge. I'm crossing here," she stated.

"No, you're not."

"Stop me." She stepped into the water. Peter gently took her hand and pulled her back. "Snake, she might have a point."

Snake looked at him incredulously. "She has open, *bleeding* wounds on her feet. You have one on your shoulder, and Rosalia . . . well, she has one, too."

Peter knew what Snake was getting at, and had to commend the man for not saying what he feared most out loud. "Emily's right. We don't have enough daylight left to walk five miles to the next bridge. Baltasar wants us in the jungle at night. He has something planned for us, and I for one don't want to find out what it is."

Snake looked thoughtful. And a touch irritated?

"I tell you what," Peter said. "I'll walk out to the bridge, just up to here —" he gestured to his chest "— and judge how deep the water is."

Snake shrugged his shoulders. "It's your call."

Peter walked into the water. He hadn't made it more than two feet when he began to feel something moving around his legs. He quickened his pace. As long as he didn't let his wound go beneath the water, he should be okay. Otherwise the piranhas would have a feeding frenzy, and there wouldn't be much of him left to ship home.

He continued walking carefully, judging each step to make sure the river bottom beneath his feet was secure. The current was strong, but he was able to walk all the way out to the bridge without the water reaching above his stomach.

"We can do this," he said as he came back to shore. "Em, hand me the baby."

Snake picked up Rosalia and held her high above the water. Peter looked at Emily and said, "Stay here and wait for me to carry you."

"But why?" she protested. "That's ridiculous."

"Trust me, Em." He could see by the guilty shift in her eyes that she wanted to trust him — it was just difficult for her and always had been.

The two men — Snake carrying Rosa,

Peter carrying Manuel — walked carefully toward the bridge. After Peter handed Rosalia the baby, he turned and saw Emily once again step into the water. Before he could say a word, her eyes widened and she jumped back on shore.

"The river is full of leeches," she screamed, then looked down at a new wound on her ankle.

"They're not leeches," Peter said as he met her back on shore. He picked her up and carried her out into the water.

"What are they?" she asked, with a tremor of fear in her voice. She kicked up her foot and stared at one particularly nasty bite. Peter watched a drop of blood fall into the water and squeezed her tighter to his chest. As quickly as he could he lifted her up onto the bridge.

"Dinner," Snake said and speared a fish with large pointy teeth and bulging eyes.

Emily blanched. "Piranhas?" she squeaked.

"Yep, pretty tasty."

She turned to Peter, a spark of anger lighting her eyes. "You let me walk into a river filled with piranhas and didn't tell me?"

"I told you to wait for me."

"Yeah, but you didn't tell me *why.*"

"I didn't want you to panic."

"I am not a child. You should have told me."

He stared at her. Maybe she was right. He couldn't expect her to just trust him blindly, without knowing what she was getting herself into. Maybe that had been part of their problem all along.

"You're right," he said. "I will no longer protect you from life's brutal realities."

She looked skeptical. "Thank you. I think."

"Don't thank me yet. Before this day is over, you might long for a little ignorance," he said, and couldn't help wondering what Baltasar had in store for them next.

Chapter Thirteen

They were so hungry the fish actually tasted good. Emily's stomach was full, but her feet ached and the sun was sinking lower in the sky; soon it would be dark. She could only imagine the nocturnal animals that made their way out at night to strike fear into the hearts of the natives.

She didn't want to see a single one.

They pushed forward, moving quicker, realizing how much more dangerous it would be to reach the lab after nightfall. Especially if Baltasar was lying in wait for them. What better way of torture than to make them walk through *his* version of paradise before meeting up with whatever he had planned for them.

Snake gestured for them to walk softly toward him. "The lab is right through there." He pointed off the road toward the right.

Emily didn't see anything different that would have given Snake an indication of where he was. "We have to go off the road?" She didn't like the whine in her voice, but over this torturous day she'd gained a great deal of respect for the road.

"Yeah, and be careful for trip wires. Step everywhere that I step," Snake insisted.

Emily nodded. Once Snake turned, Peter helped Rosalia and gestured for Emily to step behind them. Perhaps it was the skepticism on his face, but suddenly it occurred to her that Peter might not trust Snake as much as she did. But he hadn't seen how worried Snake had been for his sister, how he would rather die than let anything happen to her. He also hadn't seen how Snake had saved her life by shooting that horrible man who had pointed a gun at her.

He wouldn't be leading them into a trap. Would he?

"Are you sure this is the way?" Emily asked. She couldn't even discern a path through the thick carpet of jungle foliage. Surely if people had been stomping through here to get to some mysterious lab, there would be a path, or some sign that they weren't the only people to have set foot here in the last one hundred years.

"Shh," Peter said, and gestured with his hand for her to be quiet. She hated it when he did that.

Snake bent down and pointed to something hidden in the bushes. They all stood around him and peered through the greenery. Emily's stomach dropped. A thin wire. What would have happened if she'd tripped on that? Would she have blown up like in the movies? Or would Baltasar's guards be on them faster than she could say "there's no place like home"?

Thank goodness they had Snake.

For what seemed like an eternity, they walked carefully through the bushes, following Snake, stepping everywhere he stepped, not making a sound. She watched Peter's back. How could he live like this? He seemed to thrive on it. He didn't even notice when he came within inches of a nasty looking insect or stepped on something squishy.

Emily tried to push it all out of her mind, to focus on each step. Soon they'd be at the lab and, God willing, they'd find a Jeep. Thirty minutes later, when she didn't think she could stand the tension any longer, and she just knew Rosalia was going to collapse or the baby was going to cry and give their position away, Snake stopped. Appearing among the trees, a few ramshackle buildings became visible.

Emily swallowed. "This was it." Her eyes met Snake's.

He said something to Peter she couldn't discern.

"They look deserted," Emily whispered, and her stomach dropped as she realized there were no Jeeps in sight. If they didn't find one, would they have to spend another night in the jungle?

Peter turned to her. "You and Rosalia stay hidden here behind this tree. Don't come out for any reason, and don't make a sound."

"Peter, you can't leave us." Panic gripped her heart. "What if you don't come back? It will be dark soon. I don't want to be sitting in the dark worrying about you, wondering . . ." She looked down.

He took her cheeks in his hands and stared deep into her eyes. Her heart jumped in her throat. "I will come back. I promise."

She tried to believe him, but there was no way of knowing what he'd be walking into. There was no way of knowing if he could come back. But she had no choice but to watch him go, and pray God would protect him. "God is our refuge and strength and ever-present help in trouble," she prayed as she watched the two men walk toward the deserted lab. At least she hoped it was deserted.

The last thing Peter wanted to do was leave the women alone in the jungle while he and Snake investigated the lab, but he had no choice. Baltasar knew they were on their way. He would be waiting. They skirted the open area as long as they could, then sprinted across the clearing to the first building. This one looked like a toolshed where they found all the supplies the workers would need and a generator to fire up the lamps in the processing lab.

Peter placed his hand on the side of the generator. "It's cold."

"This is usually where the Jeeps are parked."

Peter looked at the empty area with a sinking feeling in his gut. They crept out of that building and entered the next. This one held the offices and living quarters. As Peter stared at the large bed in what Baltasar obviously used for a bedroom, he was tempted to go back for Emily and Rosalia and bring them in here. The poor women needed a few hours' sleep, but that would be foolish. Baltasar and his goons could be anywhere.

"It's deserted," Snake said.

"And the office? The computers?"

"Gone."

Peter swore under his breath. They were too late. "Other than the next building, are there any other buildings we haven't seen?"

Snake shook his head. "Only a shack at the airstrip."

Peter walked into a makeshift kitchen and opened a cupboard. He was relieved to find a few cans of food and some utensils in a drawer. "Are there any weapons stashed anywhere?"

Snake opened a cabinet next to the desk. It was empty. "Nope."

Peter shook his head. No weapons, no phone, no Jeep. Things were not looking good, and worse, he didn't like the look on Snake's face. "What is it?"

"It's too quiet."

Peter nodded. He knew exactly what he meant. "What next?"

"We should check out that last building."

"Just to make sure we don't run into any surprises?"

"Exactly."

Peter didn't like it. He took a small kitchen knife out of the drawer and stuck it in his pocket, then handed one to Snake. It was the best he could do. They watched out the window for a good twenty minutes, but saw no movement anywhere.

"Ready?" Snake asked.

Peter nodded. "Now is as good a time as any."

They crept toward the last building, walked its perimeter, but didn't hear or see any sign of movement. Finally, they went inside. The building loomed quiet in the shadows. No one could be seen hiding behind the rows on long tables. They stood inside the door. "Everyone is gone," Peter said.

Snake didn't respond but walked farther into the room.

"What is it?" Peter asked. His gut tightened as he watched Snake's furtive movements.

"Did you hear that?" Snake cocked his head listening. "There it is again."

Peter heard it now. Some sort of splashing water sound. He walked farther into the room, standing by Snake, his gaze searching the walls of the building. "Where is it coming from?" he asked.

They both stood still, listening, then at the same moment looked down.

Peter's eyes widened at the gaps in the floorboards beneath his feet, but the warning his mind screamed came a second too late. The false floor beneath them collapsed and they fell into an underground water hole.

Peter stood knee-deep in the brackish water, wiping it from his eyes and giving his head a shake. "Where are we?"

"I don't know," Snake answered. "I had no idea this was even here."

Peter tried to get an idea of the size of the underground cavern, but there was little to no light and he couldn't see much. Somehow they had to get back up into the warehouse but the floor was a good fifteen feet above them.

Suddenly they heard a splashing sound on the other end of the cavern. Peter's heart froze.

"I don't think we're alone," Snake said.

The tone of his voice raised the fine hairs on the back of Peter's neck. He shuddered to think what could be in the water with them. In a Venezuelan jungle, it could be anything.

Suddenly a light shone down through the opening above them. Peter caught his breath.

"Hello, Pietro, Snake. So nice of you to pay us a visit."

The light moved to the side, and Peter could see Baltasar and Esteban smiling through the opening.

"We heard you were on your way and went through a lot of trouble to prepare for you."

"What do you want, Baltasar?" Peter demanded.

"I want you on your back begging for mercy, Pietro."

Peter narrowed his eyes. "Not in a million years."

Baltasar laughed. "We'll see about that."

He shone the light on Snake. "I must say I'm very disappointed, Snake. I thought better of you than a backstabbing liar."

"I paid him," Peter said. "His only job was to bring me here."

"Then I'll have to thank him properly. By the way, Snake, how is your sister, Rosalia?"

Esteban snickered, and Peter saw Snake's fists clench at his side. He prayed Baltasar hadn't found the women.

"Gentlemen, I have the ultimate gift for your ultimate betrayal. I'd like to introduce you to my favorite pet, Leona, and her friends."

There it was again — a sloshing in the water. Baltasar laughed and dropped his light. Peter lunged for it, grabbed it and then shone the light down the darkened cavern. The single beam caught the sinewy movement of a giant snake moving toward them.

"Anaconda," Snake whispered.

That one word froze the blood in Peter's veins. He spread his legs, pulled out his knife, and braced himself for the impact.

Emily shivered with the approaching darkness. Rosalia's fever raged. The baby started to whimper, and the young mother pulled him tighter to her chest.

"We're going to make it, Rosalia. They'll be back soon, and then everything will be all right. You'll see." But even as Emily whispered the words, she worried that everything wasn't all right. The men had been gone far too long and it was almost dark.

Then she thought she heard something. Her heart stilled. She stared into the clearing of the labs. There it was again — laughter. A slow finger of fear crept up her spine.

They weren't alone.

The baby's distress grew. Alarmed, Emily looked at Rosalia and the baby. Rosalia was trying to quiet him, but the little one wasn't cooperating. "Here, let me try," she whispered. If Baltasar found them now, they'd have no hope. Reluctantly, Rosalia handed her the baby. Emily walked in a circle, rocking back and forth, softly cooing to the child. Luckily, the baby quieted. She continued rocking, afraid to stop, afraid of what would happen if Manuel started fussing again.

As Emily watched the clearing, she saw Baltasar and Esteban walk out of the third building . . . the building Peter and Snake had gone into. They'd been caught. Their only hope now was to make sure *they* didn't get caught, too. Emily stepped back behind a large palm frond, and hoped Baltasar and Esteban wouldn't walk toward them.

Of course, that's exactly what they did.

Baltasar was laughing, talking about Leona and there being nothing left of Pietro and Snake but the bones she spit out. His words, his laughter, froze the blood in her veins.

He was a monster. She realized that up until now she'd never believed that people could be that evil. That deep down there was a modicum of goodness in everyone and if someone could just reach that goodness inside, then anyone could be saved, anyone was worth love.

But she was wrong.

This man was evil. He'd had the sweetest, most innocent love of a child, and still his heart and soul were corrupt. Emily hated him. But worse, she couldn't see straight over her fear at what he'd done to Peter.

She turned to hand Manuel back to Rosalia, deciding to search for a large stick in case the worst possible scenario came to pass and she had to defend them. Rosalia gasped. Emily took one look at her wide, terrified eyes and froze. Not six feet away, a midnight black jaguar with yellow-green eyes crouched, staring at Manuel, its eyes focused, its muscles primed. It opened his mouth and licked its lips with its long tongue.

Emily stared at it in horrified shock.

She heard a sound behind her, and turned to see Baltasar and Esteban were heading their way. Emily's heart pounded, but she grabbed control of her fear and handed Rosalia the baby. She whispered next to her ear, "As soon as I have it distracted, take the baby and head around back of the buildings. Watch for trip wires, and don't let Baltasar see you."

Rosalia nodded. Emily gave her the baby then picked up a large branch and started swinging it over her head. *It will be okay,* she told herself. *It just wants to play with them. Baltasar always kept his cat fed, so it wasn't like it was starving and wanted dinner, it just wanted to torture us for a while.*

The cat's eyes followed the path of the branch. "Come on, Akisha. Run away," she whispered.

Rosalia touched Emily's arm. "That's not Akisha."

Emily's eyes widened. "It's not?"

Rosalia shook her head.

Emily felt the color drain from her face. Okay, maybe it *was* hungry. Maybe it did want dinner.

Baltasar and Esteban were almost on top of her. Emily didn't know where she found the courage, but she started swinging the large stick baton style, round and round while moving closer to the cat. It snarled, its paw swatting at the stick.

Emily gave Rosalia a short nod. Rosalia and Manuel disappeared into the jungle. Emily stepped back, still swinging the stick, still keeping the cat's attention focused on her, and moved into the bushes at the same moment that Baltasar and Esteban stepped into the clearing. As she had hoped, the cat's attention swung to the two men.

It snarled, and they froze.

Esteban pulled a black revolver from the

251

waistband of his pants. Emily covered her mouth to keep from making a sound, when she felt something move on her shoulder. Stiffening, she glanced behind her. The diamond head of a snake slid across her shoulder. She gasped and stared horrified at the small snake. She knew immediately it was the famous fer-de-lance, the deadliest snake in the jungle. With one swift movement, she slipped the stick under the snake and flung the slithering reptile, not caring where it went as long as it was away from her.

She swallowed a scream of disgust as it flew across the clearing and landed on Esteban. He jumped and yelled, swatting at the reptile as it slid across his back. It was all the time the cat needed to pounce. In shock, Emily watched as the cat sunk its sharp teeth into Esteban's neck. Baltasar turned and fled, doing nothing to stop the cat and save his guard. Emily turned away.

She cautiously worked her way through the jungle, circling around the buildings, trying to get as far from Baltasar as she could — hoping he hadn't heard her, or given much thought to snakes flying though the air. She had to find Peter.

Earlier she had watched them walk into the third building farthest from her. She ran up behind it, oblivious to the jungle and the creatures that brushed past her. She skirted the side of the building, listening for any sound within. Peter yelled something. To Snake? Her breath caught. She quickened her pace.

Taking one last look for Baltasar, she ran into the clearing and through the building's door. All was dark and gloomy, with nothing but the ghostly shapes of long empty wooden tables. Peter yelled again, a sound full of pain and frustration, a sound that she'd never heard before.

The sharp edge of fear sliced through her. She stepped farther into the room and saw a large hole in the floor. She ran to the edge of the hole, afraid to look down, afraid of what she'd find. Snake grunted then gave out a primal yell. Emily peered into the gloom and saw both men, struggling, fighting with something beneath the water.

Eyes widening, she strained to see into the water, her heart pounding, her breath coming in sharp and painful gasps. The water itself was moving, and it wasn't just from the waves their struggles were making. It seemed to be alive.

"Peter!" she called. He didn't answer. Couldn't. Like a warped pretzel, a large-bodied snake was wrapping itself around him, squeezing.

She had to do something! But what? She looked around her, hoping to find a rope, a ladder, anything — but other than the tables, the room was bare.

Peter let out another anguished groan and she knew if she didn't do something, he would die. Suddenly he disappeared beneath the water.

This was it!

She ran over to one of the tables and gave it a shove. It barely moved. She pushed again, but the thing was too heavy. She looked around her, but there was no other alternative. This table would have to move. Through her terror and determination, she found strength. She reached deep down inside herself, and pushed that table with everything she had, heaving it across the floor and toward the big gaping hole.

"Watch out below," she yelled, as the table crashed through the hole. She grabbed onto the end and held, sliding across the floor, hoping it wouldn't take her down with it, hoping she could keep one end anchored on top of the hole.

The far end of the long table hit the bottom with a large wet crash. Emily peered through the hole, hoping she wouldn't find Peter or Snake crushed beneath the table. Instead she found them clawing their way up, covered in blood. She held out her hand, and Peter grasped it and pulled himself up.

She threw herself into his arms, not caring that he was wet and gooey and stinky. Just thankful he was alive. He squeezed her tight then reached back a hand for Snake.

"Thanks for the save, Doc!" Snake said, as he pulled himself up and stretched out on the floor trying to catch his breath. "You do this kind of thing often?"

"Only when people I love are in danger." She looked at Peter and smiled. "So, how about we get out of here?" she said and stared out the doorway into the darkening jungle.

"You're on," Peter said. They hurried out the door and into the clearing, but no one said what Emily was thinking, no one said where they would go next, what they would do.

Rosalia was sitting against a building with Manuel in her arms. Her eyes were large, her skin pale, and Emily could see she was exhausted.

"What now?" she asked.

Peter and Snake looked at Rosalia then at each other.

"The airstrip," Snake said.

Peter agreed. "It's our last hope."

"Lead on," Emily said, and prayed the airstrip wasn't too far away. They hadn't walked far at all when they all heard the rumble of a small-engine plane.

"Hurry," Peter urged. They tried to run, but the exertion was too much for Rosalia.

"Go ahead," Emily called.

The men ran ahead, and Emily stayed behind, helping the young mother as best she could. "We're going to make it, Rosalia. You have to believe that."

"I do, Dr. Emily. We have to. For Manuel's sake."

Emily heard the scream of a cat, and shivered. It was almost completely dark now.

"Come on, Rosalia," she urged.

Soon they could see lights in the distance. They moved as quickly as they could, heading toward the lights. As they broke into a clearing, they saw a small lit-up runway and a shack off to the side, but no sign of a plane in sight. They headed toward the shack.

Peter and Snake were nowhere to be seen. "Not again," Emily muttered.

Suddenly, she heard the whine of a plane and looked up to see it approaching. "It's going to land," Emily said.

Peter and Snake came running out of the shack. "Quick, into the jungle!" Peter said, and pushed them back into the trees.

Chapter Fourteen

From his vantage point in the bushes, Peter watched the plane barrel down the runway. "What was in the shack?" Emily asked. "Nothing," Peter said. It had been completely cleaned out. They were running out of options. No phone, no Jeep, no way of getting help for Rosalia and Manuel. He clenched his hands, as the plane moved toward them. Now they had a new threat.

"Do you know how to fly?" Snake asked.

Peter shook his head. "You?"

Snake grinned. "I'm sure we can figure it out."

Emily smirked. "At least it should have a radio."

Rosalia started praying under her breath.

The plane rolled to a stop. The men pulled out their knives. The side door of the plane opened. Peter and Snake began moving, each in opposite directions, keeping hidden in the cover of the trees.

"Max!" Emily yelled.

As Maxwell Vance jumped down onto the runway, Peter's chest filled with relief.

"Yes!" he yelled and ran toward his father. They fell into a clumsy embrace as Emily, Snake and Rosalia, carrying the baby, hurried toward them.

"What are you doing here?" Emily asked. "How on earth did you find us?"

"We've been monitoring the lab for a while now through high-definition keyhole satellite images. When I saw Baltasar was here, doing his best to clear out the lab, I figured you could use a ride home."

"You figured right!" Emily gave Max a huge hug. "You have no idea how good it is to see you."

"I had a feeling you might need me, and some of Lydia's cooking."

"You didn't?" she asked, her eyes widening. She turned to Peter, and he didn't think he'd ever seen her look happier. They followed Max into the plane where inside he had a small refrigerator full of chicken parmigiana straight from the Stagecoach Inn. "Pinch me, Peter. I've died and gone to heaven."

"Then I'm there with you sweetheart." They filled their plates full of food and headed home.

"Anyone know what happened to Baltasar?" Max asked.

"We heard a plane depart about twenty

minutes before you arrived," Snake answered through a mouthful of chicken.

Max got on the radio and started talking. Emily leaned her head on Peter's shoulder. He placed his arm around her and pulled her close, thankful that they'd all gotten out of South America safe. With full stomachs and relieved minds, they all drifted off to sleep. Even baby Manuel.

Several hours later, they awoke as they were landing in Colorado Springs. Max piled them into his Suburban and drove them all to Vance Memorial Hospital. By now, they all had infections, and needed their wounds tended.

Once Peter had his shoulder stitched, and a heavy dose of antibiotics in his system, Max walked into the room.

"Rosalia's been admitted. Snake is with her and Emily is getting a few more hours' sleep in the room next to her."

"Good, she needs it," Peter said.

"It looks like you all do."

Peter nodded and yawned. "It's been a long day."

"Do you want me to see if there's an empty room here for you or do you want me to take you home? I know your mother would love to see you."

Peter smiled. "She's going to be furious at you, Dad."

"She knows there are some things we just can't talk about."

"In theory, yeah."

Max nodded. "I know. Believe me, she's been making me suffer in her own little way for the past three years." He grinned. "That's what I love about her, your mom doesn't take anything from anybody."

"Not even from you."

"Especially not from me." Max stood. "Well, come on, let me take you home. I haven't told your mother you're back yet. This way, we can both face her in the morning together."

Peter grinned and stood. He was tempted to look in on Emily, but he knew she would be sleeping. He'd come back and check in on her later after they'd all gotten more rest.

"Before we get home," Max said as they settled in the car. "I want to know what your immediate plans are."

Peter stiffened. "I don't have any. I haven't thought further ahead than sleep and food."

"Baltasar's Cessna was found crashed in the jungle."

Surprised, Peter turned to look at him.

"Don't get your hopes up. His body wasn't found."

"Perhaps a wild animal . . ." Peter said hopefully.

"No trace of anything. He just vanished."

Peter nodded. "The man is too evil to die."

"How would you feel about going back to find him? You know that jungle better than anyone."

"What about my cover?"

"How many people have seen you?"

"Just Baltasar."

Max nodded his head. "It could work."

"Is this what the Director wants?"

"He's leaning in that direction."

Reluctance weighed down Peter's shoulders. He'd just gotten home. He hadn't even seen the sunrise over his hometown yet and his father wanted to send him back. Alone.

"You know, Dad, I wouldn't have made it out of Venezuela without Snake and Emily. Without you picking us up. In fact, I don't think I would have made it out of Baltasar's anaconda pit if it hadn't been for Emily's quick thinking."

"You've managed alone for three years, Peter. When the chips are down, we're always there to help."

"I'm not sure I like the isolation. I'd always thought that I liked working solo, but now I'm not so sure." He paused. "Now, I think I like working as part of a team better."

"You mean working with Emily."

Peter thought about that. Thought about going back into the jungle without her, about leaving her behind. "I'm not sure," he admitted. "I think I'd like to stick around Colorado long enough to find out."

"You're real good at what you do, Peter. You have good instincts. You can have your job and have Emily, too."

"Emily's not like Mom. She won't sit back and let me leave her over and over again."

"Your mom had you three boys to worry about."

"We weren't a substitution for you, Dad. And you should have been around more . . . we needed you."

Max kept his eyes glued on the road. The only indication that he was distressed by Peter's words was the way he kept rubbing his face. Peter didn't want to cause problems, but Max needed to know what he'd done to their family, if he was going to understand the decision Peter was facing. "Besides, you know I can't give Emily a bunch of babies to keep her busy. I don't have that option."

"You can adopt."

"That's true. But would it be fair to the kid? To only be around part of the time? To take the chance of never coming home at all? Emily wouldn't sit idly by and make the best of the situation."

"She would if she loved you enough."

"I don't think putting up with loneliness and fear is a measure of love, Dad."

Max sighed. "What about you, Peter. What is it you want?"

"I want to feel good about what I do. I want to feel like I'm making a difference in the world. But I don't want to be alone anymore."

"Do you want Emily back?"

Peter sighed. He remembered how he felt when he saw Emily sitting up in her bed at Baltasar's estate wearing that pale pink nightgown, her hair slightly mussed and falling around her shoulders. She'd looked at him with large eyes filled with vulnerability, with longing. He'd wanted to pull her into his arms and never let her go.

Then he pictured her up above him at the mouth of that hole, her face red from the exertion of pushing that table — she'd been so brave. He'd never been more proud of her, more awed by her strength and determination. "She's an incredible woman."

"That she is," Max agreed.

"I'm not sure if I deserve her."

"Peter, she would be lucky to have you."

Peter looked at his father. "After everything she's been through, I'm not sure she still wants me."

The next morning, Peter woke to the scent of frying bacon and strong coffee wafting through the house. He took a hot shower, put on a fresh change of clothes and felt almost human again. He walked softly down the stairs and stood in the kitchen doorway for a minute just watching his mother cook.

Emotion filled him as he took in her appearance. She looked older and more tired. She turned, her eyes widening with shock and surprise as they met his. The egg whisk clanged as she dropped it on the floor. Her hand flew to her mouth, muffling a soft gasp. Her big brown eyes filled with tears. "Peter," she cried and flew across the room.

"Hi, Mom," he said, and squeezed her tight.

She drew back and looked at him, her

motherly gaze taking in every nuance in his face, her fingers tugging at his hair, the same way they had for as long as he could remember.

He gave her a warm smile, and said, "Morning, Mom. Breakfast sure smells good."

She smiled. "And you can use some, too. You're skin and bones. Come, sit down and eat."

"Yes, ma'am," he said and sat at the table. He missed her, even more than he'd realized.

"I'm not going to ask you where you've been," she started, but something dark filled her eyes as she said it. He didn't like seeing that shadow there. It was the same look she'd always got whenever their father had come home from one of his "business" trips. "I'm just going to ask if you're okay."

"I'm great, Mom. Now that I'm home."

"You planning on staying for a while?"

She wasn't looking at him, just poking at the eggs in the pan.

Max walked into the room. "I don't think he's decided yet. He's got a head-strong woman on his mind. The kind that gets under your skin and needles at you." He gave her cheek a quick peck.

She turned and glared at him, then

scooped the eggs into a bowl and set them on the table next to a platter of bacon and fried potatoes. "Anyone want toast?" she asked evenly.

Peter stood up and pulled his mother into his arms. "Sit down, Mom. I'll make the toast."

She looked up into his face, and almost cried again, but she pulled it together and gave him a small smile. "You always were such a good boy.

Peter grinned. "I love you, Mom."

"I love you, too, Peter."

Emily woke in a hospital bed. She stared at the white sheets and yellow blanket and wondered if it had all been a nightmare or if she was dreaming and would still be in the jungle when she woke.

Her friend, Kate Montgomery, stuck her head in the door. "You awake?"

"I think so," Emily grumbled. As she moved, every muscle in her body ached, then she knew it wasn't a dream.

"Want some coffee?"

Emily smelled the heavenly brew wafting through the room. "I would kill for a cup of coffee."

Kate smiled. "I thought so."

Her friend came into the room and sat

on the edge of the bed. Emily sat up and took the offered coffee. She took a deep smell and smiled before taking a drink of the hot liquid. "Ah, coffee has never tasted so good."

"What happened to you out there?" Kate asked. "I hate to say it, but you look like a mess."

"And you haven't even seen my feet yet."

Kate grimaced.

"Leeches," Emily said and shuddered. "I guess I got that adventure I wanted."

Kate groaned. "Did I mention Adam wants to go back?"

"No way!"

Kate nodded.

"How are you with snakes and spiders?"

Kate's eyebrows rose. "Well, they don't send me screaming for the hills."

"Cats?" Emily asked.

"I love cats," she replied.

Emily smiled. "Then you should be just fine. Just remember, there are a lot worse things in the jungle than snakes and spiders."

Kate furrowed her eyebrows. "Okay, I'll keep that in mind."

Emily laughed at her skepticism. "By the way, how is my friend, Rosalia?"

Kate's face darkened. "She's not good, Em."

Emily's heart sank. "What is it?"

"Sepsis. It's raging through her body. The doctors are doing their best to fight it."

"I knew she needed antibiotics, but there was nothing I could do." She shook her head. "We just couldn't get her here quick enough. First that horrid man with his grenade launcher and then we ran out of gas. It was just horrible."

Kate stared at her wide-eyed, then shook her head and patted Emily's knee. "She's a fighter, Emily. We're all praying for her."

"And Manuel?" Emily was afraid to ask, but her friend gave her a wide smile.

"He's perfect — healthy, strong, a good baby."

Emily blew out a relieved breath. "Thank the Lord."

"You did a great job."

"Thanks, I surprised myself. I did all kinds of things I never thought I could do before. I delivered a baby! When that precious little life slipped into my hands, it was the most beautiful thing I'd ever seen, the most joyous moment I've ever had."

"You'll have a baby of your own, someday," Kate assured her.

Emily looked grim. "I hope so."

"I know so. You'll make a terrific mom."

"And you'll make a terrific godmom."

Kate smiled and leaned forward to hug her. "I've missed you."

"You, too."

They both took a deep swallow of their coffees. Then Kate lowered her voice conspiratorially. "Is it true? Is Peter back?"

Emily nodded.

"And are you two . . . ?"

She shook her head. "I thought we might be for a while there, but God opened my eyes."

"Oh?"

"I know that Peter is happy doing what he does. I don't think he's the type to ever settle down and raise a family. I realize that now, and trying to force him to live in a box wouldn't make either of us happy. It just wouldn't work."

"Oh," Kate said, obviously surprised. "I'm sorry to hear that. I always thought you two were perfect for each other."

"Don't get me wrong. I love Peter. I just realize now who he is. And I love him enough to let him go. I'm ready now to get on with my life, to move forward and put the past behind me. To put Peter behind me." But even as she said the words that sounded so logical, so confident, an ache grew in her heart and she knew her life would never be the same. There would always be an empty spot in her heart that only he could fill.

Kate sighed. "Well, then all in all, I guess this trip was good for you."

"It was a nightmare — a living, breathing nightmare. But I realized as I moved from one adrenaline rush to another that I've been living in limbo for too long, waiting for something that would never happen. It's time to move on, to reclaim my life, to figure out what it is I really want."

"Are you sure that it's a life without Peter?"

"I don't think I'll ever be sure about that, but I saw him almost get blown up. I saw him wrestling with giant anacondas. The man carried me through a river full of piranhas."

Kate's eyes widened.

"He liked it. He needs excitement in his life. He needs danger. He needs that constant adrenaline surge and now that I have those pictures in my mind, I will never be able to sleep at night wondering where he is and what kind of danger he'll be facing next."

"Security is one of life's necessities."

The door shut softly and Emily's eyes widened. "Was someone there?"

A few seconds later a nurse walked into the room.

"Was someone just in the hall?" Emily asked.

"A tall, dark and extremely handsome man," the nurse said, grinning. "Though he didn't look happy."

Emily's eyes widened as they met Kate's. *Peter.*

Emily shot out of the bed.

Peter strode down the hall. What had he been thinking? He'd let himself believe, even hope, that he and Emily had a future together. That he would be able to change his whole life to fit her into it. To make her happy. But he'd been wrong. She'd already moved on. She couldn't be happy with his life, no matter what changes he made. She'd always be wondering if she was making him happy. If she was enough. She'd always be wondering if he wanted more.

He heard his name being called down the hallway. He stopped and turned. Emily was running toward him. He steeled himself, not wanting her to see how upset he was. Not wanting her to know how close he'd come to falling back into the same old trap. She could never love him the way he needed to be loved, with all her heart. Not holding anything back.

"Peter, stop," she said as she reached him.

He looked around him. "Em, you're standing in a public hallway in a hospital gown."

"It's all I had," she said, looking down at her bandaged feet.

Her face was sunburned and peppered with bites, but he didn't think she'd ever looked more beautiful. The thought squeezed his heart.

"Did you hear what I said to Kate?"

He nodded, not trusting himself to speak.

"I'm sorry."

"Don't be. It was something I needed to hear."

"You made it very clear to me in Venezuela how you felt about us. That we didn't have a chance, we couldn't make it work."

"You're right. We can't."

"I understand that, intellectually. It's my heart that's having a hard time believing it." She looked up at him with those wide, hazel eyes filled with emotion, and he wanted to pull her into his arms, to convince her they could make it work. That they did have a chance.

But he couldn't. What if he was wrong? He couldn't go through losing her again. "If we were to try again, it would only cause both of us a lot of pain when it fell apart. Nothing has changed. You still don't trust me to do what's best for us. We're still the same two people we were three years ago."

"The same two people who still love each other," she whispered.

"I can never give you what you need, Emily."

She moved closer to him. "I'm not sure what it is I need anymore."

"Security, family."

"Quit the CIA, Peter. Stay here with me."

"And do what?"

"I don't know. Join your brother's security company, be a cop."

"I'd still be in danger."

"That's true, but I know something now that I didn't know three years ago."

"What's that?"

"How good you are at your job. You were born for law enforcement. It's in your blood. You will never be able to give it up and be happy."

He looked down at her in surprise.

"I want you to be happy, Peter. I just want you to be happy here in Colorado Springs with me."

"There's more, Em. I haven't told you everything." Her forehead crinkled with concern. "What is it?"

"The explosion three years ago . . ." He rubbed his hand down his face, then just blurted out the words that had been eating at him for the last three years. "I'm sterile. I can't give you children. I can't give you a family."

Her face went ashen as his words sunk in. He turned and walked away. She didn't come after him. He didn't look back.

Chapter Fifteen

Emily's heart sank as she watched Peter walk away. *Sterile?* She looked down at the ground trying to process what he'd told her. The secret he'd kept buried from her for all this time. That was why he didn't come after her when she'd left him at the hospital three years ago. That's why he folded so easily and let her divorce him. She thought he hadn't loved her, that he'd loved his job more.

But he'd been letting her go.

The same way she was letting him go now.

He'd loved her so much, he'd let her go thinking it was best for her, thinking she'd be happier. But he'd been wrong. What if she was wrong, too? She took a deep breath to call him, but before she could move, she felt someone touch her arm.

"Emily."

She turned to find Kate staring at her, her eyes filled with sadness.

Emily's stomach lurched. "Kate, what is it?"

"It's Rosalia. She's . . ." She didn't finish, just shook her head.

Grief squeezed Emily's heart and her throat tightened with tears. She followed Kate down the hall to her friend's room, and tried to prepare herself for the worst, tried to steel her emotions, but it was no use. She was too physically and emotionally spent. She'd seen too much, felt too much to be able to cocoon herself from her emotions.

She opened the door and walked into the room. Snake had Rosalia's hand clutched in his. His head was bent over it and his shoulders were shaking. With one look at Rosalia's face, Emily could tell she'd come too late. Tears spilled onto her cheeks.

She placed a comforting hand on Snake's shoulder. He looked up at her with such pain and anger in his red, swollen eyes that she almost stepped back. Instead she stepped forward. "What can I do?" she asked softly.

He shook his head. "There's nothing."

She pulled up a chair and sat next to him for a long time, neither of them saying a word. She thought back to how hard Rosalia had fought to have Manuel, to stay alive for him, to love him. She recalled the unwavering trust and love she'd held for her brother. She'd been an admirable woman and Emily was proud to have known her.

"Baltasar did this," Snake said, gritting his teeth. "He is going to pay for killing my sister."

Emily understood his anger and wished she could think of something to say that would help him. There were no magic words at a time like this. The best thing she could do for him would be to listen, to let him get out all the anger and sadness.

"I will make sure Manuel grows up despising the name Baltasar Escalante," he said. "He will know everything his mother did to protect him from that animal, all she gave up and how much she suffered."

"Hopefully by the time Manuel is old enough to understand, Baltasar will have been locked up in jail for a very long time." She touched his arm. "Rosalia would want her child to be happy, to live without hate and anger. Don't give Baltasar that much power. He doesn't deserve it."

Snake considered her words, then nodded. "You're right. It would be better if Manuel never heard Baltasar's name. And Baltasar will never know he has a son. A son who doesn't know he exists."

Emily's eyes widened. Of course, why

hadn't she seen it before? A shiver coursed through her as she stared into Snake's dark eyes. "If Baltasar ever finds out about Manuel . . ." She couldn't complete the thought.

"He would take him, I know."

Emily stared at Rosalia's hand still clutched in Snake's.

"He can't ever find out, Snake."

"Don't worry. He won't. I will protect my nephew. I will do what's best for him. I will do what my sister would have wished."

Emily left Snake's side and went up to the nursery. Manuel was lying in his bassinet, wrapped tight in a blue swaddling blanket and wearing a matching blue cap on his head. "Hey there, big guy," she said to the baby. Her throat tightened as he looked up at her with his big, trusting brown eyes.

"I'm so sorry, baby," she whispered. She thought about the hard road ahead of him without his mama and with a madman for a father. He deserved so much more. Tears filled her eyes and fell down her cheeks. "Your mama loved you so much. She was a brave and special woman. A great mother," she said, and took a deep breath to try and gather her emotions. She lifted the baby out of his crib and hugged him tight, hoping that somehow, some way, he would get all the love he deserved.

"How's he doing?" Snake asked, walking up behind her.

She smiled through her tears and handed him his nephew. "He's a trooper."

"He's Manuel DeSantis. He has the strength to overcome. He is a fighter."

Emily smiled. "He is blessed to have an uncle like you."

Back in her room, she found a pair of jeans and T-shirt that Kate had left on her bed and quickly changed. She was a fighter, too. And right now she had a lot to fight for.

Emily took a deep breath and rang the bell of the Vance house. She was determined to put things right, once and for all. They'd wasted enough time, enough love. Each doing what they thought was best for the other, but neither giving consideration of what was best for themselves.

Peter opened the door. He didn't seem surprised to see her.

"Did you really think I'd care?" she demanded.

"How could you not? A baby is all you've ever wanted."

"No, Peter. *You* are all I've ever wanted.

How could you not know that?"

He looked stunned. He stepped out onto the porch and shut the door behind him.

"We need to stop thinking so much and just feel," she said. "How do you feel about me, Peter?"

Pain entered his eyes, but he made no move to touch her. "I love you, Em."

"What do you want?" she asked, wishing he would pull her into his arms.

"I'm not sure."

"That's a problem."

"I know I don't want to live without you."

"That's a start." She smiled.

"What about you? What do you want?"

"I want to be involved in your life. I want to know what you're doing and where you are. I want to share everything with you. And if we're blessed enough to find a family along the way, then that would be perfect."

"I'm not sure where things stand with my job. I'm not sure I want it back, but I'm not sure who I am without it."

Emily nodded — she understood but she also realized that was something he needed to figure out for himself. "Rosalia died today," she said softly. "She had her whole life ahead of her and now it's gone. She's lost so much. I don't want to lose any more time."

Peter nodded as sadness filled his face. "How's Snake?"

"Consumed with hate and grief. Life's too short, too precious to waste. I don't want to waste any more time without you. Give it some thought, okay?"

He nodded, his face grim.

"I'm going home to take a long, hot, much-needed shower."

"All right." He bent down to give her a kiss.

Once his lips touched hers, she pulled him to her and savored the feel of him next to her. This was where she wanted to be. She didn't want to lose him. "I've missed you," she said. "It's good to see you home." She turned and walked down the drive. The ball was in his court now. He knew how she felt; their future was left to him.

"Emily," Max said as she started to get into her car.

She stopped. "Hi, Max."

"Peter told me what a great job you did in Venezuela. How you really came through for him."

Emily smiled as her heart filled with delighted surprise. "Oh, I don't know about that. I think he thought I was more a pain than anything else."

Max grinned. "Peter used to think he could take on the world alone. Now he knows better."

"Is that right?"

"Absolutely. In fact, the CIA could use someone like you out there, someone who's fierce under pressure, someone who can keep her head when the sky is falling."

"Oh, yeah," she laughed. "I think you got the wrong girl, Max."

"I don't. I think you and Peter would make an incredible team."

She looked at him with quiet speculation. *A team.*

A short time after midnight, Peter woke. He lay still, listening in the darkness. He'd heard a faint sound, but couldn't determine where it had come from. He slipped from the bed and glanced out the window. Something woke him, someone was out there. Had Baltasar discovered who he was? The quiet street looked deserted.

He continued to watch out the window. Nothing moved in the halogen glow of the street lamp below. All was clear. He shook his head. There was someone out there. He could feel it.

"Don't move a muscle," a voice whispered in his ear.

"How'd you get in here?" he whispered.

"Turn around real slow, hands in the air."

Peter whirled and hooked his foot beneath the intruder, knocking him off balance and pushing him to the floor. He flung himself on top of him, grabbed his wrists and pinned them above his head. He stared down at the figure in black beneath him and pulled back the black ski mask.

Peter choked on the startled breath caught in his throat. "Emily!"

She smiled wide. "Hi, handsome."

"What are you doing? How'd you get in here?"

"Right under your nose, Mr. CIA man," she said smugly.

He let her go, then sat up, stunned. "I don't understand. Where have you been? I haven't seen you in over a week."

"Max felt I could use some training."

Peter's eyes narrowed in suspicion. "What kind of training?"

"You know — weapons, ballistics, stealth, what have you."

"You mean breaking and entering."

"Without ever being seen. I guess I passed, eh?"

"Emily, this isn't funny."

"Isn't it?"

"No." Peter stood, and started pacing the room. He couldn't get his mind to function, couldn't get the image of her dressed in black, pinned beneath him, out of his mind. What if he'd hurt her?

Emily stood. "Max thinks we'd make a great team."

"Really?" His father was in serious trouble.

"Yes."

"Em, I can't imagine what has gotten into my father's head, and I'll deal with him later. Please, sit down." He sat on the bed and patted the spot next to him.

She shrugged, then sat. "This week while you've been gone, I've been doing a lot of thinking," he began.

"Oh, yeah?"

"I don't want to live without you. Not anymore. Marry me, Em. I'll give it all up. I'll leave the CIA. I've already talked to Travis about joining him at AdVance Security. Just say you'll give me another chance."

She looked at him, her big eyes luminous and beautiful. "I can't."

His heart sank. "Why not?"

"Because, Peter, you're good at what you

do. You love the CIA. You might be happy at AdVance, maybe even for a year or two, but then you'd look around at your life here in Colorado Springs, and you'd hate it. Then you'd begin to hate me."

"Emily, I could never —"

"I won't let you quit the CIA. It's not just a job to you. It's in your blood. It's what you do. That's why I've decided to join you."

Peter stared at her. "You can't be serious. What about the hospital? Your job? Your life here?"

"I can use my expertise in the field. I want my life to be with you, wherever you are. My training has just started, but after a few months I will be ready to join you. Until then, maybe you can stick around and give me a few pointers." She gave him a wink and a smile.

"Oh, yeah?" He moved closer. "What kind of pointers did you have in mind?"

"I need to know how to bring a man down. Why don't you show me that little move you used on me earlier?"

As Peter stared at her, his face broke into a large grin. If she was serious, this could really work. They could really work. Maybe he'd be thanking his dad after all.

In the next few days, the Vance household was a flurry of activity as everyone got ready for Thanksgiving Dinner. As Emily was helping set the large dining room table, she heard the doorbell ring.

"I'll get it," she called, and hurried through the living room to open the front door. "Snake," she said, surprised as she saw Snake standing on the porch holding Manuel. "Come in. How's the baby?" she asked and stepped aside so they could enter.

"He's great. A lot of work, but great. Want to hold him?"

Emily nodded. "I'd love to." She took Manuel from his arms and held him tight, breathing deep his sweet baby smell. He looked up at her with his big brown eyes, and she couldn't help wondering if he remembered her. "He's getting so big," she said happily. "You must be doing a great job with him."

"Thanks," Snake said. "Actually, he's why I came by."

"Snake," Peter said, walking into the room. "What's up?"

"Mind if we sit down?" Snake asked.

"Please," Peter gestured toward the couch.

Emily couldn't stop looking at Manuel. He was so beautiful. So little.

"I was wondering how you would feel about adopting Manuel," Snake said, looking from Emily to Peter.

"What?" Emily asked concerned. "But you're doing such a good job with him. He loves you, I can tell. He already recognizes the sound of your voice."

"I love him, too," Snake said. "And I want to do what's best for him. I want to give him a real family, a happy home. You have that here." He gestured toward the huge dining room table set for eight.

They did have a family, a large and loving family. "But, Snake," Emily protested.

"I'm going back to Venezuela, and I don't want to take him with me. I want a better life for him."

"But why go back?" Peter asked. "My dad is having citizenship papers drawn up for the both of you. You can start a new life right here."

"And always be looking over our shoulders, wondering when Baltasar would show up and steal Manuel? I can't take that chance. I'm going after him. It's the only way to keep Manuel safe."

Emily understood his logic, but her

heart broke for him. "I love this baby. You know that. You know I would never let anything happen to him."

"I know," Snake said. "That's why I brought him to you. I know you can give him a good family."

"We will never let him forget who his mother was or about his brave uncle Snake."

Snake looked down and Emily could see he was trying to control his emotions. "Thank you both," he rasped.

Max entered the room, and they explained the situation to him. He agreed to have the adoption papers processed and delivered by noon the next day. They invited Snake to stay, but he took one last look at Manuel and left.

Emily's heart broke as she watched him go. He was such a good man, but he'd given Baltasar everything he'd had.

"This could be a problem," Max said.

Emily's heart sunk. "What?"

"Baltasar knows who you are. He knows you were with Rosalia. If he finds out she was pregnant and gave birth to Manuel, he will know where to find you and the child."

Panic rose in her throat and she pulled the baby close to her. "Then what can we do?"

Peter smiled. "Dad, don't scare Emily like that. I know exactly what you're up to."

"What?" Emily demanded, wondering if she should be scared or not.

"He has an assignment for us."

"What kind of assignment?"

"A safe assignment. An information-gathering assignment. It's in France. You can go as a family. We'd give you papers, change your names — there is no way Baltasar or anyone else could track you down."

"For how long?" she asked.

"As long as it takes."

Emily looked to Peter. "What do you think?"

"I think as soon as you complete your training, we get married and make this official."

Laughter bubbled in her throat and she looked down into Manuel's face. "Really?"

Peter leaned forward and kissed her long and hard. "Really."

The doorbell rang again and Vance family members started pouring in. Emily sat on the couch looking stunned, holding tight to Manuel as Peter greeted his brother, Sam, and his new wife, Jessica, and Jessica's adorable little girl, Amy.

The newlyweds were both beaming.

"What is it?" Peter asked.

"We're expecting," Sam said, and patted Jessica's stomach.

Peter couldn't have been happier for them. "That's great," he said, and hugged them both.

He turned to Emily, but she was still sitting on the couch staring at Manuel, as if she couldn't believe he was really there, and really hers. Peter hoped everything would work out. He knew how much she loved that baby.

Max walked in from the kitchen, carrying a tray of mulled cider. "I thought I heard the sound of more Vances."

"Yeah, and expect more in another eight months, Dad. Your Vance clan is growing."

Max beamed. "Congratulations, both of you." He thrust the tray into Peter's hands and patted Sam on the back. "I knew you could do it, son. I had faith in you."

"Thanks, Dad," Sam said with a smirk.

"A toast," Peter said, passing around the cider.

"To what?" Travis asked as he and his new wife, Patricia, walked through the door. The former college sweethearts had been recently reunited during their own Diablo/La Mano Oscura investigation.

"To dreams coming true," Emily said from the couch. She stood and took her glass.

"Who's that?" Lidia asked from the kitchen doorway.

Emily smiled and walked over to her. "This precious little guy is Manuel DeSantis-soon-to-be Vance."

"What?"

Emily nodded, and tears filled her eyes and ran down her cheeks. Peter's heart overflowed. His mother hugged her then held out her hands to the baby. Emily placed Manuel in her arms.

"He's so beautiful," Lidia cooed.

Peter turned his attention back to Travis as he heard him mention Jake Montgomery. "He's working on the information you gave him now. The files you downloaded contain further evidence to cement the case against Alistair Barclay as the head of the Diablo crime syndicate."

"Good," Peter said, but he wished he felt like he'd accomplished more. He wished Baltasar was the one in custody, the one facing trial. As long as he was out there, none of them were safe.

"They're gearing up for Barclay's trial in the next couple weeks," Travis said.

"This will be a big one for Jake," Sam

added. "It will be his biggest case to date, and it will help him launch that political career he's been dreaming about."

"What Jake needs is a good woman by his side," Lidia said, giving Emily a warm smile. "With a good woman, a man can accomplish anything."

"You'd better believe it," Max agreed, wrapping his arm around Lidia's waist and giving her a squeeze.

"Come to the table, dinner is almost ready."

"Smells good, too, Mom," Travis said with a large smile.

They all chatted as they headed to the table, but Emily hadn't budged. Peter went to her. "Is everything all right?"

"Not yet."

"Why not?"

"Because you haven't held your son."

Peter stared at the baby in her arms and realized she was right. He hadn't wanted to think of Manuel as his, he hadn't wanted to believe that everything was coming together for them. That finally they'd get everything they'd always longed for. He held out his arms and stiffened when she placed the baby into his hands.

"He's so small," he said, looking down into the baby's eyes.

"And strong. Relax, he won't break."

Peter smiled, as joy filled him. "Our son," he said, a little awestruck, and when he looked up into Emily's eyes, they held a fine sheen of happy tears. They walked into the dining room and stood at the head of the table. "We have an announcement of our own we'd like to make," Peter said. "The Lord has sent us a message."

"Oh, yeah. Now he talks to God," Travis said, laughing.

"He has," Peter insisted. "He has made my life —"

"And mine," Emily added.

"Miserable," Peter finished. "Because we didn't stay on His path."

"And if there's one thing we've learned over the last few weeks," Emily reiterated, "it's to never veer too far off the cobblestone path."

Peter smiled, and pulled Emily close. "So now that we're back on track, Emily and I are getting remarried."

"Hear! Hear!" Sam said.

"It's about time," Travis agreed.

"Not only that, but Travis, I'm going to have to turn down your job offer, because Emily and I are going to be working for the CIA, together."

"What!" Lidia cried, standing. "What about the baby?"

"Yeah, what about the baby? Who is it?" Travis asked.

Peter turned his son to face his family. "Everyone, I'd like you to meet Manuel DeSantis-soon-to-be Vance."

"But if you take him with you, when will I see him?" Lidia demanded.

"You'll see him. I promise," Emily said, and hugged Lidia close. "Bonjour, Mama," she whispered in her ear.

Lidia smiled, understanding Emily's unspoken words. "Then I have an announcement I want to make, too."

"Oh, no," Max groaned.

"I've decided I want to go to Europe for the summer holidays," she announced and smacked Peter's hand as he tried to reach around her to steal a roll. "France," she said as she looked at Max. "What do you think?"

Max sighed. "I think a Vance has to do what a Vance has to do."

"But if at all possible," Peter prompted and gave Emily a quick kiss, "never do it alone."

Dear Reader,

I truly enjoyed writing this story because it's about forgiveness and having faith in God's plan. Emily has forgotten that the Lord knows her better than she knows herself. Even though she feels alone in the world, the Lord hasn't forsaken her. "For a brief moment I abandoned you, but with deep compassion I will bring you back." (*Isaiah* 54:7)

Her journey through the Venezuelan jungle is filled with obstacles and hidden dangers, but along the way she renews her faith. She and Peter rediscover their love for each other and realize that all that is missing in their lives is faith — faith in the Lord and faith in each other. They find their way back to each other by staying true to God's plan and by not letting fear push them off course — "blessed is he who trusts in the LORD." (*Proverbs* 16:20)

I hope you enjoyed reading Emily and Peter's journey in book five of the FAITH ON THE LINE series. Be sure to look next month for the final story, *Protecting Holly*, by Lynn Bulock.

I'd like to thank the other authors in this series, Gail Gaymer Martin, Carol Steward, Felicia Mason, Kate Welsh and Lynn Bulock, for their support and guidance on this project. I'd also like to thank Jeff Sweetin, Special Agent in Charge of the U.S. Drug Enforcement Administration for his expertise. All exaggerations and inaccuracies are mine.

Cynthia Cooke

About the Author

Cynthia Cooke — Ten years ago, Cynthia Cooke lived a quiet, idyllic life, caring for her beautiful eighteen-month-old daughter. Then peace gave way to chaos with the birth of her boy/girl twins. Hip-deep in diapers and baby food and living in a world of sleep deprivation, she kept her sanity by reading romance novels and dreaming of someday writing one. She counts her blessings every day as she fulfills her dreams with the love and support of good friends, her very own hunky hero and three boisterous children who constantly keep her laughing and her world spinning. Cynthia loves to hear from her readers. Visit her online at http://www.cynthiacooke.com.

The employees of Thorndike Press hope you have enjoyed this Large Print book. All our Thorndike and Wheeler Large Print titles are designed for easy reading, and all our books are made to last. Other Thorndike Press Large Print books are available at your library, through selected bookstores, or directly from us.

For information about titles, please call:

(800) 223-1244

or visit our Web site at:

www.gale.com/thorndike
www.gale.com/wheeler

To share your comments, please write:

Publisher
Thorndike Press
295 Kennedy Memorial Drive
Waterville, ME   04901